Freewhee[illegible]

Life, love and cycling around the Lakes of Killarney

and beyond

Máire O' Leary

978-1-912328-90-1

Published in Ireland by Orla Kelly Publishing.

To my husband Ger and my two wonderful boys Odhrán and Rían. Without you all, this would never have happened.

Acknowledgements

To my mom who fostered my love of books, instilled a strong sense of self-belief and taught me to stick with the journey as long as it takes. To my husband Ger who has listened, encouraged and supported me through the many false starts. To my two beautiful boys - 'it's true your mom really wrote a book'. Since your arrival you have taught me so much; patience, acceptance, joy and most of all the depth of a mother's love.

To the Ring of Kerry and Ring of Beara charity cycle organisers, I salute you for the work you have selflessly put into those two amazing events over the years. I pledge 10% of the profits of this book to be shared equally between two charities you regularly support, Kerry Rape and Sexual Abuse Centre, Tralee and South West Counselling Centre, Killarney.

To all of you who have shared my life so far "thank you", it has been a privilege. A special thanks to Noreen McGrath for your inspirational gift that mobilised me towards the final completion. To the strong, inspiring women I am surrounded by at my day job, it's true what they say "if you see it, you can be it" many of you are truly inspirational. To Martin Grogan my colleague, the first person I knew who wrote a book; your experience made me think, if he can do it then so can I.

To all those who have helped with this project in any shape or form, I thank you sincerely, especially the 'Bantry Ladies' and the 'IT Tralee Sisterhood'. To my sisters, Niamh, Cáit and Fiona thank you for your endless hours of proofreading and plot development. To Lisa Daly, thank you for the use of your stunning photography. To Jeremy Murphy of JM Editing and Orla Kelly of Orla Kelly, Publishing I thank you both for your professional support.

To you the reader, thank you so much for choosing to read this book, I hope you enjoy it, and if you do, please tell your friends.

CHAPTER 1

Our world is beautiful…all we have to do is open our eyes

It's that time of year again, it's March, the evenings are getting longer. The bikes are beginning to appear on the road. On her way home from work Saoirse passes three cyclists and begins musing. Will I do it again this year or can I actually be bothered? It's a lot of miles over the highways and byways of Kerry. To be fair there are not many highways and truth be told, I have a preference for the byways.

As these thoughts run through her head they are quickly followed by ones of long fine evenings on her bike where it's easy to let go and pedal along roads with the sun shining and a gentle breeze blowing. The countryside is laden with scents, like the sweet aroma of flowering currant, that beautiful bush with the pink flowers, or better yet the honeysuckle. Oh, the honeysuckle, that sweet summer smell that just makes you want to stop and breathe it in long and deep. Then there are the mornings, now they really are the best. Leaving the house at 7am and just heading off and letting the road and bike take you where it will. The beautiful clear clean morning air. Usually with no one else around apart from the odd sheep on the road or cow or horse looking over the hedge. For Saoirse it's her version of heaven. These are mornings worth living for. It's like the world and the roads are just made for her to enjoy the strength and power gained from many years of training.

Then Saoirse thinks of the day itself, the atmosphere, and the build up to the first Saturday in July, the Ring of Kerry Charity Cycle. It's the day that thousands of cyclists set off from Killarney to conquer the majestic Ring of Kerry. Pedalling along all you can see is the colours and carnival of thousands of cyclists full of joy and enthusiasm. For many it's the culmination of their efforts having conquered personal challenges to be a part of this epic day. All while raising funds for their chosen charity. The feeling of anticipation is palpable as cyclists depart Killarney. The sense of community and craic[1] is immense throughout the day, never mind the shared high and sense of achievement that is felt at the finish line. She would argue with anyone that it's the best day out on the Kerry calendar. It is an event on the Kerry social calendar that truth be told she is unable to resist. Not alone for the day itself but also for the banter in the lead up to it. There really was no decision to make, she would be on her bike heading for South Kerry on that first Saturday of July at 6.30am with all the rest of

1 Irish colloquial way of saying fun

the cyclists. She would also sign up for some other events like the Ring of Beara to help with her preparation for the main event as she saw it.

At 29 years of age pushing for 30, Saoirse is a tall, athletic brunette at 5 foot 8 inches, pretty face, striking brown eyes and a body that most women would die for. It had been honed and toned through years of sport and physical activity along with a relatively good diet. With her life of exercise she has always had some leeway with food and is partial to the odd treat. As she says to herself, no harm in a bit of what you like. Activity for Saoirse is just a way of life, it's not a chore or something she has to do. She just loves the great outdoors. She grew up on the football field and loves the feeling of being alive that comes from a gruelling training session, where a good rewarding sweat has been worked up and there is the gentle soreness of used muscles.

She is a strong, independent woman, well able to look after herself, and successful in her career as a health coach. She has however one gap in her life, she has trouble finding Mr. Right. Her friends have told her it was her own fault, because they say, once anyone gets too close, she pushes them away. Saoirse likes her independence, her life as it is, but she acknowledges its the fear of what that commitment can lead to, that is the problem for her. Having grown up with a domineering mother she has learned the value of her hard-fought freedom and has no intention of giving it up lightly. Also having watched some of her friends struggle through the transitions of motherhood, from pregnancy to birth and beyond, the prospect also terrifies her. She acknowledges for some they are fulfilling their life's dreams and even then, it's hard. But for other free spirits like herself she has seen what the ravages of sleepless nights and sick children have brought. Saoirse is certain she is not ready for that kind of life change or commitment right now... She acknowledges though, that if the right person came along maybe her opinions would change, life is, after all, a journey with twists in the road.

All the heavy stuff aside, Saoirse had grown up addicted to romantic comedies and while she wouldn't readily admit it, she dreams of falling in love with the tall, dark and handsome stranger. However, she would settle for someone athletic, fun and kind-hearted. Saoirse would love some romance in her life, to feel her heart flutter with attraction and to have someone special to do things with. Her ideal guy would treat her as an equal, respect her as a woman, be amazing in bed and definitely would not be looking for a replacement for his mother to do his cooking and cleaning. She is not auditioning for that role.

Just as she turns in the gate to home, she shakes herself and says enough of the day-dreaming, pull yourself together and be thankful for the life you have. You have a good, well-paid job. You have a beautiful home that you can afford to pay for. Her house is a three-bed cottage with white walls, black around the windows and a red door. As a small child she once passed a similar house and decided if she ever owned a house it would look like that house but it would also have a garden like one of her old neighbours, with a manicured lawn and beautiful flower beds. Sitting in her driveway she acknowledged that she had fulfilled the dream of house colour, but the garden was a different matter. Little did she realise the work that would go into making that dream a reality. If it hadn't been for her Dad and Oisin's help she knew it would never have happened. Gardening she learned is a full-time occupation, especially if you don't really know what you are doing and tend to kill off half of what you plant. But not one to give up easily, she has kept at it and it's beginning to take shape, although it's still a serious work in progress. One old timer once said to her that "a garden is never complete, a beautiful garden is one's life work" and she is beginning to believe him.

After six years of trial and error she has partially mastered the seasons, in spring it is a mass of colour with all sorts of daffodils, tulips, crocuses and snowdrops. In late summer it's magnificent with gladioli, sunflowers, sweet peas and roses. It's the bit in the middle that is the challenge but maybe this year she will get that sorted. If only there were something with bulbs that would keep coming back themselves, she wistfully thought. This business of planting every year is not really for her, although she does like messing about in the small tunnel that she has out the back in spring. It's a great sense of satisfaction when you plant a little seed and see it reappear a few weeks later.

Opening the door into her rustic cottage and breathing in a sigh; "home sweet home" she says out loud to no one in particular. Her beautiful little cottage is the love of her life with its timber finishing and old fashioned dining table and chairs. She loves her Stanley stove that once lit sends out a glow of heat around the cottage and makes it so comfortable and cosy in the winter. It really is her escape from the world, the perfect place to come home to and just chill out. The agenda for the evening, to grab some supper and then out to the garage to get out her bike to see what sort of a state it is in after its winter of hibernation.

First she has to clear the way into it and remove the buckets, spades and all the other gardening paraphernalia that are in the way. On reaching the bike she realises that tonight will not be the first training night after all. At a glance it looks like the tyres are flat and they are probably a bit bald as well, the chain could do with a bit of oil, all of which she could sort out herself but then this will be its 5th ring and the cogs for the chain could also probably do with replacing. What was she thinking anyways, that after sticking it in the garage for the winter she could just hop on it and head off? She decides that at lunch tomorrow she would take it to the bike shop and let them look it over and then she wouldn't have to worry about something coming loose while careering downhill or having a breakdown on one of the many roads in Kerry that have no phone coverage. Decision made, she hauls out the bike and sticks it into the back of her car in preparation for its remodel tomorrow.

Since she can't go for a cycle, she figures her best option is to call her friend Oisin to see if he is around and interested in going for a walk with her. As she picks up the phone she wonders what his escapades from the weekend are going to be. They met a few years back playing on a tag rugby team and over the years they built a good friendship. They have a loose, easy friendship and when they are both around and not in relationships, they hang out together. As far as Saoirse knows he is free at the moment, but after the weekend who knows? There had been some football shindig on and Oisin being Oisin could have picked up a woman at it. She often wonders how their friendship works because other than their shared interest in the same activities of walking, cycling and sport some of their values were at odds, particularly when it comes to their attitude towards relationships.

Oisin is always in and out of relationships and has no bother picking up women, whereas Saoirse doesn't really bother. From her point of view he treats women like objects and once he gets sick of the latest conquest he just tosses that woman aside and moves onto the next one. She sometimes wonders what would happen if he met someone and got a taste of his own medicine. How would he handle that? Not that it matters because it means with his short lived relationships he is around a fair bit and she has someone to spend time with who is good fun to be around. She pops off a quick message *"you around this evening ..... how about a walk?, the Demesne to Ross Castle at 7."* That should do nicely she thinks, about an hour of a walk to clear out her head after the day's work. As she is clearing up after her supper of boiled egg and brown bread the phone beeps with his text. "*See you there at 7 so.*" She quickly changes into her comfortable leggings and runners and heads off into town.

Oisin saunters up to the gate with a big smile on his face and with his usual opener of "Saoirse girl what's the craic?" Oisin is tall, brown haired, blue eyed, athletically built with strong shoulders and with well developed bum and thighs or, as Saoirse puts it, a GAA player's body. He is a former footballer, who had a seriously hot head on the pitch but is generally a relaxed, easy going, down to earth guy off the pitch. As they wander along they chat about this and that, their days at work, his weekend and this fabulous woman he met from Galway. "You would love her Saoirse, she was some craic." "I'm sure" she replied "sure aren't they all." "No this lady was special." "Will you see her again?" "Yeerah no, that would be too much hassle, up and down to Galway." "Enough said so ..." Saoirse began, " ... what was she down for?" "There was twenty of them down on a mad hen weekend, I ran into her in Scott's bar and met them again later in the Grand. They were a real sound crowd and the craic was brilliant." As he rambled on about the weekend Saoirse is only half listening. She is observing the majestic scenery which she never gets sick of looking at no matter how many times she sees it. The National Park is one of the real advantages of living near Killarney. As they walk down through the centre of the park towards the river to head for Ross Castle along the lake shore Saoirse takes a deep breath and thinks this is really God's own county. Imagine the privilege of having this on your doorstep on a fine March evening with the leaves just starting to come back on the trees, the beautiful blue lake with Tomies mountain in the background. It really is such a magical place. Taking another deep breath she just feels the days tension seep out of her shoulders as she relaxes and he continues to ramble on about the weekend.

After about 20 minutes she says, "By the way I have decided to do the Ring again this year. You know for me it will be 5 in a row, are you up for it?" He hums and haws saying, "I don't know it's only the first week of March. I won't be making a decision on that until at least the end of April. Sure that's not on until the first week in July, there is plenty of time to think about that. If I am and that is a big if, I won't be doing anything until at least the end of April or start of May." "Alright, no need to eat me I was only asking were you going to do it? I am not asking you to make a big life decision like to marry me or anything." Wistfully she says, "But just think of flying down the hill from Moll's Gap, or heading out through the trees by Muckross on a beautiful Sunday morning with the sun and the blue of the lake flashing through them." He comes back with, "Or what about when your thighs and calves are burning and you have run out of grub, it's pissing rain and you are moaning 'Why do I do this to myself?' How about that for a picture or have you forgotten that one?" Saoirse goes into a huff even though she has a sense that he is just pulling her leg. "Ah Oisin, why are you trying to kill my buzz on this?" Oisin replies, "I am not, I am just trying to give you a dose of reality, how many times did I have to listen to you last year? What about when your calves are so tight that you have to go to the physio to get them dry needled and you can hardly walk to the car afterwards?" "Ah shut up they are just the bad days and don't we always say no pain no gain? Anything worth achieving requires a bit of work and there are more fun days than rough days. Anyways my mind is made up I am going to do it. I have the bike pulled out and I am taking it in for an overhaul tomorrow. I will start doing a little bit of training from next week and you are welcome to join me if you want, but if you have better things to do then no pressure."

They wander along together in comfortable silence for a while, each lost in their own thoughts while taking in the scenery that surrounds them. Oisin wonders to himself how is it that he has no problem spending time with Saoirse even though he seriously thinks she could relax a bit? Everything with her is always so planned and she rarely goes with the flow. In the evenings, after a busy day, she is often wound like a coiled spring ready to burst. God help the poor fella that ends up with her and has to deal with her on a daily basis. Not for him, he prefers his women more relaxed, although she is a good friend and is always there to listen to his tales when he needs someone. He thinks it's amazing that once she is out in the fresh air for a few minutes he can see her begin to visibly relax, her shoulders drop, she begins to smile and is usually ready for a laugh and a bit of banter.

To Oisin's way of thinking, you can't get any better form of healing than fresh air, a fine evening, a bit of exercise and good company, and if you're lucky, some decent countryside to experience all of that in. In fairness to her, for all his mocking about whinging and whining Saoirse is a great training partner. Once she puts her mind to something she rarely gives up. She just grits her teeth and gets on with it. You would have to admire that in a woman. As they round one of the final bends on the path the castle finally appears through the trees. It's an impressive sight with the flat calm water in the foreground, the purple heather mountains behind it and incandescent evening white light forming a halo over the castle. Saoirse catches his arm saying, "Oh! Oisin just look at that. Wow it's breathtaking this evening, I wish I brought my camera with me. Did you bring your phone Ois? That is some photo." "Ah Saoirse why can't you just appreciate it for what it is?", he asks. "Not everything needs to be captured through a small screen you know." Recently Oisin had become increasingly annoyed with everyone's need to capture everything they did. He couldn't understand why they couldn't just enjoy it but he said, "I must admit though, it's fabulous alright."

As they approach Ross Castle they can hear the laughter of children and families who are out feeding the ducks in the little stream beside the castle. They walk around the front to get away from the noise and sit down by the little jetty and relax, letting the sound of the water lapping off the lake shore flow over them. After some time Oisin says, "come on we had better be getting back before it gets dark." Reaching out his hand he pulls her up from the bench, holding it for a little longer than was necessary, quickly letting it go when he realised.

CHAPTER 2

Exercise invigorates us; all we have to do is move

With her bike back in action and a couple of short cycles under her belt, or lycra so to speak, Saoirse decides to take on the Gap and give the legs a good test. The Gap is a 35 mile round trip from Killarney and one of the most testing cycle routes near the town. It is a series of hills and dips through wild, rugged countryside with beautiful, untouched scenery. It has it all, sheer sided rocky mountains, rivers, lakes, and hidden mountain valleys dotted with small farms here and there. As the weather forecast was predicting a fine morning, followed by heavy rain in the afternoon Saoirse decided to head out early and get back before the rain. She calculated that if she left around 8am, she should make Moll's Gap and the Avoca cafe for 10am. She hoped they would be open, because at the top of that hill there is nothing like an Avoca fruit scone with homemade raspberry jam and cream and a good cup of tea. It's pure heaven, and like the old saying goes "hunger is a great sauce."

As Saoirse heads off on the first leg of the route, the easy part to Kate Kearney's Cottage, she decides to take it easy and not push too hard, just loosen up the legs and warm up the body in preparation for the hills to come. This was, after all, her first significant cycle of the year. It's a fabulous, crystal clear morning with some birds chirping away here and there, and as it's Sunday, cars are a rare sight on the road at this hour. The air is clear and as she opens up her lungs and warms up her legs on the bike she feels free as a bird with nothing or no one to bother her. Cycling from Kate Kearney's to the head of the Gap is absolute bliss; there are no obstacles to negotiate, no walking tourists or jaunting cars (the local horse drawn traps that transport the tourists up and down through the Gap on a daily basis). The road is her own apart from the solitary sheep grazing at the edge of the road.

Onwards and upwards the winding road takes her past the first lake and the second lake, both of which are nestled into a valley surrounded on both sides by sheer mountains strewn with boulders and intermittent cliff faces, a regular haunt of rock climbers and other adventure-seeking climbers. The mountains just seem to rise straight out of their reflection in the lakes which are perfect mirrors on this calm morning. On this route she often wonders about the farmers who live here and how they make a living, particularly in the past when people had to live off the land without subsidies from Europe or a job off the farm to supplement their income. They must have had many hungry days as it's nothing but rock and bog. Growing potatoes in a place like this must have been a hardship, but grow them they did, and there is still evidence of the old potato fields here and there today. As the road rises she spots the massive boulder halfway out across the road that signifies the first real, steep climb. This is the first test of her training; if she can make it to the top to the bridge above the boulder then her training will have paid off. She turns the gears down in preparation and gets ready to stand and pedal. As she climbs, turning pedal by pedal towards the bridge, her thighs and calves begin to burn, her heart is hammering in her chest and her breathing is fast and shallow, but she vows that even if it kills her she is not getting off the bike. She has done it before and knows she can do it again; she just needs to dig deep and keep going. She is not now or never has been a quitter, so she will make it. With sheer grit and determination she pushes herself to the top and throws the bike against a rock, bends over with hands on her thighs to get her breath back and to control the shaking in her legs. To herself she makes a mental note that a bit more hill training is required before she will be ready for the Ring. While there are no hills with this gradient on the Ring, only a couple of long ones which are usually doable if you have the work put in advance, it makes the day itself so much more enjoyable if you are not struggling up the hills. After a few minutes her body returns to normal and she is ready to get a drink of water from the bottle.

Once she has regained her equilibrium it's back on the bike and along the flat part of road beside the lake. She loves this part of the road as it flattens out as it passes along beside an old derelict farmhouse. There is a new road surface which makes it easy to cycle along here. She is fast approaching the next climb which rises over a series of bends in the road, and as you circle towards the top you get a fantastic view back down the valley below. It must be a geography teacher's Mecca with its glaciated valley, river and ribbon lakes. At this hour of the morning it's peaceful and quite without the tourists that arrive in their bus loads to walk the valley and have coffee in Kate Kearney's Cottage, a traditional bar that always has the fire lighting and usually has an eclectic mix of tourists, locals, hill walkers and cyclists. At the head of the Gap she decides that she will hop off her bike and enjoy some peace and quiet, have a banana and a chocolate bar to build up a bit of energy before taking on the Black Valley. Saoirse believes that while these cycles are training, they should be enjoyed, and she believes in stopping at regular intervals, so she always takes routes with nice cafes on them. Tortuous rides where you just ride for two or three hours straight without any break are not for her.

She is looking forward to the next leg of the route, which is a fast down hill into the Black Valley past the church. At this hour of the morning, she should be able to let go of the brakes and enjoy the thrill of the hill without worrying about having to slow down or stop for any obstructions in her path. There is nothing like freewheeling down once she makes the corners at the bottom and watches out for any local drivers speeding up the road against her. The downhill is her reward for the uphill climbs, it's just a pity they can't last longer. She passes the little church on her right where a few years ago she and her friends on a walking trip took shelter to eat their lunch. It's a pretty little rural church and not a bit pretentious. Onwards she heads into the valley itself along the flat, through the bogland area where the turf will be cut and reeked later in the year.

At this point, you can see the Killarney to Kenmare road to the left above as it winds its way through the mountain side, although this is her destination for her pit stop, she doesn't know if it is a good thing or bad thing that you can see it because it never seems to get any closer when you are down below in the valley pedalling along. Looking up, she notices that the sky has turned an ominous grey. As the Avoca coffee shop above on the Killarney to Kenmare road comes into view, she realises there are no lights on. Oh no she thinks, this is just bloody perfect, I'm too early for the coffee shop and the rain is coming in fast over the mountain, I am going to get drenched and be starving at the same time. She begins her silent mantra of 'please, oh please let it be open by the time I get up there and please let me get up before this rain starts'. As the morning starts to go against her, her mood is gradually darkening with the clouds that are sailing in overhead. She curses her foolishness and wonders what the hell brought her out here at this hour of the morning, why couldn't she be like most normal 29 year olds at home in bed tucked up with a fine hunk of a man after a good Saturday night out? But then she remembers that she doesn't have a husband, a partner or boyfriend. The self-pity really begins and she is ruminating on why she can't meet someone, what is wrong with her, she couldn't even pull a fella for a one night stand even if she tried, not that she is really into that anyways. She gives herself a mental shake and says conserve your energy for the next climb you amadán,[2] you might even have to go all the ways back to Killarney without a bite of grub, so no point wasting energy feeling sorry for yourself. It was your decision to come out here, so get on with it.

She pedals on with one eye on the coffee shop waiting for the lights to come on until the road takes it out of sight. That is probably a good thing because out of sight is out of mind and she can concentrate on the next climb into the hills that will bring her up onto the Sneem road and ultimately to her destination. She normally likes this

---

2 Irish word for fool

part of the cycle because she often thinks that it would make a great spot for a movie setting. It's bleak rural countryside, undisturbed by electricity lines and poles. She could imagine something with a rugged mountain farmer or something along the lines of a western being shot here. It would be perfect. Again, she has to gear down and climb although it's not as steep as earlier, but it can be just as difficult as energy levels are running low, hunger is setting in and her legs are getting tired. It's a slow gradual winding climb of a mile or so up to the flat on top where she will be able to take a break. Her motto is it's best to keep climbing on the uphill and avoid breaking momentum no matter how slow you are going because once you stop its hard to get going again especially on a hill.

At the top she takes a moment's break to look at her watch and realises that it's 10.05am and maybe, fingers and toes crossed, the cafe will be open. As she rounds the corner the first of the rain begins to fall but she spots the lights on and the doors open and feels like jumping off the bike and doing a little dance. Now she will be able to go to the toilet rather than having to squat behind a rock somewhere. She will also be able to get a cup of tea and that mouth-watering scone. She almost kisses the waitress when she gets to the top of the stairs and smells the beautiful aroma of homemade food. She is always promising herself that she must come back here some day for lunch when she is not on the bike so she can sample some of the other luscious food they have on display, but she will have to leave that for now otherwise it will be out over the handlebars before she is down passed Ladies' View.

After refuelling, she gazes out the window at the rain sheeting down and wonders to herself will I just call Dad and get him to pick me up from here or will I brave it and head back out into the elements. Then she remembers Dad would probably be in mass at this hour on a Sunday morning. Then, he would be going to get the paper for his weekly read. He always says 'Why read the newspaper any other day of the week when you get all the news together on a Sunday?' Anyways, he probably left his phone at home as well because as he also often says, 'Sure I keep the same routine everyday so if there was a real emergency and someone really wanted to contact me they would know where to find me.' He can't understand all these people who practically have their phones as extensions of their fingers. His favourite saying is 'what did we do before phones'? 'We made arrangements to meet someone and then turned up on time. Sure, these days with all the phones and everything people still can't be on time.' Saoirse decides that she had better brave the weather and just get on with it. It's only 20 miles back into Killarney anyways and a good portion of that is down hill, how bad can it be?

Just as she prepares to leave two men arrive at the cafe in cycling gear looking for a bit of sustenance as well. As she goes to pass them out the door one guy says, "looks rough out there, where have you come from this morning?" Saoirse in her own mind wonders is this a chat up line or is he just being friendly, but she goes along with the conversation anyways. He is tall, probably 6 foot, athletically built in the rower or cyclist sort of build, sculptured shoulders, narrow lean waist and long muscled legs. He has a strong, handsome face with a striking jawline and brown eyes that you could lose yourself in. Saoirse gives herself a mental shake and says for God's sake girl he is only making small talk. Stop losing the run of yourself or he will think you are some sort of a lunatic if you don't answer the question instead of standing there gawking at him. As casual as she can be with a glow of embarrassment climbing up from her neck from her wayward thoughts, she says, "up from the Black Valley what about ye?" Gorgeous answers "Round from Kenmare, we decided to keep it simple today and just do the distance rather than the hills. Fair play to you taking them on this early in the season, we don't usually bother with that torture until closer to the Ring." "Ah well I just thought that I would see what was in the legs as a baseline and then I would have something to build my training on. Enjoy the food, see ye around, I suppose I better get back out there, the sooner I start the sooner I get home."

Saoirse hops on her bike and heads down the hill, into the wind and the lashing rain. Her mind is on the fine hunk of a fellow she had just been talking to and she wonders what his story is. Based on the get up and the quality of the bikes outside she would have thought they were fairly professional cyclists. No cheap cycling gear on them, only the best but then, if they are only doing the Kenmare run, and they don't really do the Gap, then they can't be pro-cyclists. With the body on him she would have definitely thought he was a serious cyclist. Well you can't always judge a book by its cover, but whatever he is into it certainly did his physique no harm. She pondered about him having a girlfriend and assumed he did. There is no way that, that hot bit of stuff is not attached, Probably, has some young fit, leggy blond at home, catering to his every whim. Hot men my age are never interested in women their own age, she mused, total commitment phobes the lot of them. Instead they are only looking for a good time and a bit of fun. 'Well don't be coming knocking on my door in 10 years time when you decide to grow up, because I won't be waiting around for you', she muttered to herself. She shook her head and reminded herself that she should not be tarring all men with the same brush as she was sure there was some decent lads still out there. This ripped god might just be one such lad, looking for a kindred spirit to pedal the roads of Kerry with every weekend. She would happily step up and into those shoes if he cared to ask.

Well at least that little diversion has shortened the road a bit because when she looks up she realises that she is nearly down past Ladies' View and she didn't even notice that flat part of the road near the lake and the run down house that she normally hates. She keeps the bike at a steady pace on the way down as it's not a morning now for speed, with all the water that's flowing down the road, and she is soaking wet herself. She can't believe how quickly the conditions changed from the beautiful crystal clear morning she started out with to the torrential downpour that she is out in now. Although only the beginning of April, this morning felt more like a day in summer with the thunder. She is so wet that the water is running out of her shoes and gloves; as for her clothes, they are completely drenched. Just beyond Galway's bridge she hears a hissing noise that has nothing to do with the road; 'Oh please God don't let me have a puncture in this weather,' she pleads with the universe. All I want to do is get home and into the shower to warm up. She pulls the brakes to try and stop the bike, but it just goes into a slide aquaplaning off the road in under the trees. She is on the verge of tears wondering, what am I going to do now, please, please don't be punctured. As the bike comes to a stop, she peers at the back tyre through the blinding rain. Her worst fears are confirmed, sure enough, she has a puncture, and she won't be going anywhere else until she sorts it out. As she takes out the phone to make a call she realises that there is no coverage, she can't call anyone, she will have to deal with it herself. She flings the bike and her helmet to the side and gives the back tyre a kick in a fit of rage; she then slumps down the ground under the tree and starts to cry. She is tired, cold and now she can't even call someone to pick her up. What the hell is she going to do? The bloody bike is useless and she can't ride it or fix it, and with all the technology it's let her down when she most needs it. What is the point in having a mobile if you can't use it in an emergency? With this weather there aren't too many others out on bikes that might help and anyways they will be coming down off the hill too fast to even see her. She just gives up and sits there and bawls her eyes out due to frustration.

Donal and Gerry head back for Killarney having eaten their fill in the cafe and are not too concerned about the weather. In fact it exhilarates them as they ride this route regularly, but today's conditions present a different challenge, in particular to their balance and their ability to ride at speed, negotiating the bends and keeping the bike on the road as its slick from the rain. They are flying downhill for Killarney when Donal thinks he sees something under the trees out of the corner of his eye. "Hey Gerry man", he yells over the sound of the wind and rain and water splashing under the tyres. "Pull up there will you I think there is someone under the trees back there. Based on the colour I think it's another cyclist.

What was that girl wearing that we met in Avoca?" "Ah Donal I don't have a clue man, you were the one that was flirting with her. You know I never notice things like that." "I think it was a red top and if it was, then that's her alright back there under them trees. We had better go back and check to see if she is okay. There are no other amadáns out in this rain and you wouldn't see her from a car," Donal shouted. Gerry thinking this is another one of Donal's mad ideas, off playing the hero, says "never mind man, she is just probably sitting it out for someone to come get her." "Well my mother didn't rear me to ignore damsels in distress and I couldn't have it on my conscience all day, so I am heading back up, are you coming or not?" Gerry says "no man the game is on telly in another hour and I want to be back home to at least see the second half, so I will head on and leave you to it." "What if she is badly hurt?" "She won't be, I am telling you she is just waiting for a spin, I know women and they always take the easy option." "Well I am going back up to check, I will see you later in the week, right."

CHAPTER 3

Respect, trust, kindness the ingredients of a good relationship

After a tough pedal back up the hill through the deluge coming down against him Donal finally arrived at the spot where he glimpsed the flash of red. Sure enough it was the girl from the cafe and she is hunched up and shivering with her head between her legs and he could hear what he thought was sobbing. "Hi there" he says, "we meet again, are you alright?" She looks up with a big puffy face and her hair matted to her head and says, "Do I look like I am alright? Would I be sitting here bawling if I was alright? Jesus, he thinks to himself I must be mad, to think I came all the ways back up here and this is the reaction I am getting, so much for trying to help. He says "Now you look here, there's no need to take the head off me, I just came back up the hill because I thought I saw someone who might need some help. If my presence is pissing you off that much, I can leave again and you can sort out your own sorry mess." "Alright, Alright" she says with a ghost of a smile as he turns to leave, "sorry let's start again, the back tyre on the bike is gone, I think it's a blow out and while I have a tube I don't have a tyre or patches, my phone is not working, I am frozen and soaked and unless I walk there is no way of getting back into Killarney" at this she started crying again.

"That's some list of misfortunes alright, but have you got a thumb?" She gave him an odd look, and thought, what a strange question? She says "how's that going to help me, it certainly won't plug a hole in a tyre." "No" he said "but it might have gotten you a lift if you went out to the road and stuck it out." "Yeah right" she says, "who is going to pick me up in this condition? I would soak their car and I could have gotten picked up by any sort of weirdo … On that point, how do I know you are alright? And by the way where is your friend?" He replies, "To answer point one, I think you're safe enough with me in your saturated state and in these weather conditions my intentions are honourable. As for point two, my friend felt you were just waiting for a spin home and he had better things to do than come back up here to check to see if you were alright." "Oh, so I suppose I should be thankful at least one of you is a gentleman and didn't leave me out here to perish." He sits down under the tree with her and declares "well at least you came off at a good spot where you had a bit of shelter." She turns to him and says, "Aren't you Mr positivity? How are we going to get out of this mess?" "Oh so it's 'we' now is it?" he says and smiles. Despite being miserable, soaked and frozen she felt her heart begin to beat faster as awareness and attraction reasserted itself now that she was out of imminent danger and she knew he would at least help to get her out of this pickle. Looking at him she thinks, wow that's some smile, he really is a handsome bugger, cool as you like. She says, "Well you are still here aren't you so I assume if you came back and I didn't frighten you off with my first attack, you are not going to leave me ... By the way, I am Saoirse and you are?" "I go by Donal O'Leary he says in a mock Irish American accent, how can I be of service to you maam." She bursts out laughing at the ridiculousness of the situation, stranded under the trees in the lashing rain and having this incredulous conversation with a stranger, albeit a very handsome and kind one. Shaking her head, she says to herself, wait until I get home and give Margaret a call! This is the stuff of romantic movies or novels. He says, "That's more like it, glad to see you can see the funny side in this ... by the way, I think I have some patches in my pack so we can see if we can get you a temporary patch that will take you down far enough to call someone to come and collect you."

Between the two of them they make the bike roadworthy, although it was difficult to get the patch to stick because of the wet. "I don't think that will take you back to Killarney, but it should get you down far enough to make a call. I will stay with you until you get a chance to phone someone. I assume you have someone to call?" "Christ, what sort of a loner do you think I am that I would have no one to call?" she replied. To himself he thinks this one is one prickly female, how do I find them, why couldn't I mind my own business, and now I wouldn't have to escort this one out of trouble. Being careful with his words he says "Well you could be from out of town for all I know and not have anyone around and if I am not mistaken unless you had a fight with whoever you started out with, aren't you cycling on your own today? Not many women do that. Don't you know half of the roads around here have no coverage on them? Is that really a smart thing to do?" "Oh please save the lecture, of course a woman can cycle on her own if she chooses to? This is the 21st century and although I joked earlier about being picked up by a weirdo all the statistics show that a woman is much more likely to be attacked by someone she knows than a random stranger. Anyways that lecture is one for my Dad to give me when he comes to collect me.'

Rather than getting into another argument with her he says, "we better get going while the tyre has some air in it."

After making their way down the road a bit Saoirse took out her phone and called her parents' house. Her mom answered. "Hi mom, is Dad home?" Saoirse asks straight away. "Isn't that a nice greeting for your mother," her mom replied. "Look I haven't time for this, I have a puncture and I need him to come to get me." Her mother launched into a lecture, "How many times have I told you not to be riding that bloody bike around the country and I suppose you are out on your own again?" Her mother rolls her eyes to heaven and thinks dear me, where did I go wrong? Why couldn't I have raised a lady for a daughter besides a tomboy like the one I have, she will put me in an early grave with worry. Saoirse breaks into the silence, "Look Mom, is he there or not?" "He is not here", said her mother, "he is still out at church or reading the paper in the car somewhere." "Will you come and get me so?" "Saoirse, love" her mother says "don't you know I am in the middle of getting the Sunday dinner and I can't leave it to spoil ... I will send your brother out for you, where are you anyways?" "By the time he gets here I will probably be down by the carpark for Dinish Cottage so if he pulls into that carpark, I will meet him there, he does know where that is doesn't he?" "Of course he does ... Wasn't he born and raised in Killarney the same as you?" To which Saoirse muttered under her breath, "that doesn't mean he knows where it is." To her Mom she said "Will you tell him bring some cardboard or a plastic bag so I can sit on it as I am soaking and make sure the boot is empty so I can put the bike in it. Thanks Mom" Saoirse says and hangs up.

Hanging up the phone she could feel the tears again as the emotions of the fairly simple conversation began to overcome her in her tired and wet state. Why can't my mother be supportive? Why do I have to be such a disappointment? Couldn't she have just turned off the pots and come and got me this once. As her lips began to tremble Donal put his hand on her back and said, "It's OK, we can make it down, I will stay with you until he arrives." She turned to him and with a watery smile she said, "thank you, let's get going."

Back down safely in the carpark where she had scheduled to meet her brother Saoirse turns to Donal and says, "Thanks so much for getting me out of that spot of bother back there, that's your good deed for the day complete." "Ah don't mention it, anyone would have done the same in my position. I couldn't let you out there although I was tempted with your first response," he joked and smiled that charming smile again. Saoirse noticed that he was in no hurry to leave yet he was soaked to the skin as well. "There is no need for you to hang around and catch your death of pneumonia, my brother will turn up of that you can be sure, or my parents would kill him," she said. "You are drenched and need to get home too." She decided that she had nothing to lose at this stage, he had seen her at her worst she might as well go the whole hog and invite him for a drink some evening, worst case scenario he could only refuse but he didn't seem like a guy who was into playing mind games. She guessed he was a yes or no man and she could deal with that. Jumping straight in she said "Donal I would like to thank you properly for helping me out this morning with a bit of grub and a drink but since we are in no condition to go in anywhere today how would you like to meet up some evening during the week after work?" Donal, a man never to refuse an offer of food and what he expected would be good company in a better situation, replied, "Sure why don't I give you my number and we can take it from there or, you know what," he paused, "instead of messing around with texts in this rain I am free on Thursday if you are around?" Inside Saoirse was punching the air and doing a little dance. Thinking wow that was easy, she was wondering why she hadn't taken the initiative more often in the past instead of waiting for men to ask her out. After all she is a 21st century woman in every other aspect of her life, so why has she been a shrinking violet, sticking with old fashioned customs instead of taking the plunge herself when it came to dating? Because she knew in her heart of hearts it's a lot easier to be the one to reject an offer rather than to be rejected.

She grounds herself and in a surprisingly confident voice she asks, "How about the Porter House so at seven, Thursday, that way we can get both food and a drink?" He responds with a "yeah that would be grand." In his own mind he is thinking sure there is no harm in this, she seems like a sound sort of a girl and it's only a thank you, not a date.

Donal had taken a self-imposed sabbatical from women after he found his former girlfriend of four years had been cheating on him with a work colleague. At the time he was getting ready to propose to her and had thought that their relationship was rock solid. It had cut him to the core; how she could do that to him. It had taken him a long tough year of mental torture, picking apart every aspect of their relationship wondering what had been reality and what she was faking. Initially he had found his escape in exercise; it was mind numbing, he would push himself to his physical limits and feel no mental pain while doing it. He acknowledged that truth be told, he had developed an unhealthy dependence on it. For a couple of months, running, cycling, swimming, doing triathlons and generally pushing his body to the limit was a break from his own mind. That had all come crashing to a halt when he got an injury to his right knee and lower back from overuse. The injury was the turning point; he had to face up to what he had been running away from. Linking in with his local counselling centre had provided him with the support he needed and helped him to work through the breakup. It provided a relief to the circular conversation that had been on-going in his head, thus relieving the mental torture he had been going through, and that had really helped. They had literally thrown him a lifeline that had given him his life back. Despite however turning most of the corners with the help of a counsellor, he still hadn't been out with a woman in the best part of a year and didn't know if he could ever trust another one. Anyways he told himself no need to panic, this wasn't a date, it was only her way of saying thanks. He could accept that, couldn't he? Despite the conditions of their meeting he had enjoyed Saoirse's company once she thawed out. He supposed that, if he was honest with himself, he found her both interesting and attractive, so it could be a pleasant evening. "See you Thursday at seven Saoirse" he said as Sean, Saoirse's brother, pulled into the carpark. "Thanks again Donal I'm looking forward to it already."

Saoirse is on a high as she jumps into the car with Sean having loaded the bike in the boot. She greets him with a cheery "Hi." "What has you in such good form and the state of you? I thought you would be like a dog after being stuck out in this?" "Well Seanie, it's like the old saying goes 'every cloud has a silver lining' and I certainly saw the silver today." "This guy came back for me and helped me out and now I have a date with him Thursday evening. Can you imagine that? Pulling a fellow on a morning like this. Never mind that, he seems really sound and sooo cute, not one of them gobshites that just wants to play head games with you. It's been one strange morning." "Not to burst your bubble Saoirse, but on more mundane matters, where am I dropping you off? To home or to your own place?" "Ah my own place of course, I need to have a good warm shower and change and then I will call over to Mom for the dinner … I assume it's stuffed roast chicken as usual?" "Well you know Mom is a creature of habit, she is not going to change at this stage of her life, is she?" "God Sean, I wonder if we are going to turn out like that too, so predictable, same dinners on the same day every week, do the same thing every day never doing anything spontaneous?" "Well some people find comfort in predictability, you know spontaneity is not for everyone and I think the two of them are happy out in their own routine." "Isn't that all everyone wants at the end of their days, is to be happy." "Ah for God's sake Sean, you would swear they have one foot in the grave by the way you are talking and they are only in their early sixties. They have plenty good years left yet, but they should be out making the most of it." "Who are you to judge? As I said I think they are happy with their lot and isn't that more than can be said for a lot of people."

****

Calling her friend Margaret on Monday Saoirse says "I really need some sound female advice … I have a sort of date on Thursday and I need to get something to wear that will make an impression but not look like I thought too much about it." "Right," Margaret begins, "there are a few paradoxes in that 'a date that's not a date', and 'something new to wear but that doesn't look like you got something new or made a bit of effort … Maybe start at the start and tell me the story and then I will see if I can help." Margaret is a contradiction in that she is really arty and creative, with an excellent eye for colour, fashion and style, but it's underlined with a practical no nonsense straight-talking nature. Saoirse reflected how her straight-talking has always worked for them in their friendship and they have known each other since they sat together in primary school. Saoirse knows she is the right woman to assist her on her current mission of becoming fabulous, but an understated fabulous of course. "Margaret to be honest, this is actually a thank you dinner and not a date," Saoirse explained reluctantly. It was a small fact that Saoirse had to keep reminding herself of. She wanted to look well but without looking like she has gone over the top with effort. She knew that one hour of Margaret's shopping expertise would be better than all week shopping by herself.

"Oh Saoirse do tell all," coaxed Margaret. "Well Sunday morning I was out for a cycle and having my cupa in Avoca when in came two other cyclists. One lad was really gorgeous and when I was leaving, we just shot the breeze a little. The usual cycling chit-chat like, you know. The weather had turned atrocious and I still had to get back to Killarney so I didn't really hang around too long chatting to them. Long story short, on my way down I had a tyre blow out that I couldn't fix and I ended up stuck under the trees with no phone coverage and feeling very sorry for myself. Next thing your man from Avoca is standing there in front of me. I couldn't believe it."

"Cool out he says 'Hi there, we meet again, are you alright?' or something like that. I don't know if it was the relief or the thought that he was mocking me but I was a total bitch." Margaret laughed "that would be you all right." "Anyways," Saoirse continued "once we got over our bad start, he turned out to be really sound. He patched up the bike and we made it down to the car park for the Meeting of the Waters. He actually stayed with me until Sean came for me, in the pouring rain. He was so sound. I plucked up the courage in the end to ask him to come to a 'thank you dinner' and he agreed. It was really old school, I don't have his number or anything, so I really hope he actually turns up" she continued anxiously. "I think he will though as he didn't seem to be the type to be playing games, he was just gorgeous and genuine and he saved my life. Well maybe the saving the life bit is a bit dramatic but you know what I mean." "Wow" Margaret replied "that sounds like a plot line for some soppy romantic movie" "I know that's what I thought as well," said Saoirse. "You are into him though aren't you?" asked Margaret. "To be honest I found him really attractive but I need to keep it in perspective, this is just a 'thank you' dinner although who knows maybe it might be the start of something." Saoirse said wistfully.

Margaret agreed to meet Saoirse at lunch time to go shopping as she wasn't around in the evenings. Joe, her husband, was away with work and she had to pick up the children every evening this week. She is delighted for Saoirse but in her Miss Practicality way she warns her not to get her hopes up and lose the run of herself by expecting too much. Not wanting to see Saoirse make a fool out of herself she decides to point out a few facts. "By the way, how do you think he sees this dinner? Is it as a date or does he just think he is going for a friendly no strings attached dinner with the girl he rescued off the side of the road? Do you even know what his relationship status is?" Saoirse, a bit miffed that Margaret was killing her buzz despite having asked her to keep her grounded, replies snarkily, "Well the answer to both your questions is I don't really know, I didn't specify that it would be a date but I assume that if a woman asks him for a drink and dinner that he should know it's a sort of date or potential to be a date. I actually don't know if he is in a relationship or not, but I also assume he wouldn't go out with another woman if he was." "Saoirse" Margaret says "I think you need to be careful, that's a lot of assumptions and don't you know the saying about assuming things 'never assume anything because it makes an ass out of you and me'. Men don't read into things the same way women do, believe me he most likely just thinks it's a friendly thank you, free dinner. Let's look at it another way if you went to this dinner with Oisin would it be a 'date'?" "Ah Margaret that is different, of course not, we are just friends." "All I am saying is don't go in expecting too much or you may be disappointed." Saoirse felt totally deflated when she hung up, she had been going around on cloud nine all day until she rang Margaret. No better woman than Margaret to give her a dose of cold water and bring her back to reality, she thought. Saoirse wondered for once in her life why couldn't Margaret have left me carry on with my fantasy, but she supposed it would be better for her in the long run not to go in with any expectations and she had asked Margaret for her help after all. She could still justify getting a new outfit though, and despite all Margaret's practicality she was an excellent shopper, so she was looking forward to the trip.

After hanging up Margaret was replaying the conversation over in her head and was thinking, maybe I was a little bit too tough on Saoirse. She loved her as her best friend, but she acknowledged that for such a self-confident and accomplished woman Saoirse could be so immature and a little socially challenged when it came to men. She seemed to get very intense and totally carried away initially, usually scaring the prospective guy off and if he stuck around for a while she generally pushed him away herself, except of course Oisin. Oisin was the only exception to all that. He was the only one she had never ran off and they have been 'friends' for years, Margaret reflected. At the start of that relationship, Margaret had a vague recollection of Saoirse wanting a bit more, but it had never materialised and they seemed very happy in each other's company as friends. In some ways Margaret assumed that Oisin might be part of Saoirse's problem with other men. Although friends, they had a pretty intimate relationship and a lot of other men throughout the years had been challenged by this friendship, and in truth Margaret couldn't blame them. She could never tell herself if Oisin and Saoirse were really just friends as they claimed, or was their relationship something much deeper, something they simply hadn't woken up to themselves. In Margaret's opinion you couldn't find a couple more suited to each other. Anyways thought Margaret, at least she has something in common with this new guy and he sounds nice and down to earth, so maybe she is on to something here. If she doesn't get too intense on him at the start, then maybe there is potential if he is unattached.

Thursday came around and Saoirse was distracted in work all day. She couldn't concentrate on anything worthwhile. She was supposed to be drafting a presentation that was due, but she really couldn't get it together. She decided to abandon that task and just clear out her desk which she had been meaning to do for ages but hadn't got around to it. At least that is a completely brainless task that will allow her mind to wander instead of having to concentrate. She was thinking about what she has seen about Donal on Facebook. He seems to be a really active person; most of his photos were of races or triathlons. There were also a few of other social events as well, like weddings or parties. In those he had cleaned up exceptionally well, he had looked amazing, especially those killer brown eyes and that long, lean muscular body in what looked like well-tailored suits. There was also some of him with another woman, but his status said single. For now, she is going to assume that he is single despite what Margaret said and that the lady in the photograph is his sister or maybe just a friend. Hadn't Saoirse herself gone with Oisin to a few weddings when neither of them had a date?

CHAPTER 4

Often we regret, not what we have done, but what we have failed to do

As soon as 5 o' clock came she was out the door flying with an air of anticipation. Her evening plan was: head home, water her plants in the tunnel, get a shower in, lather herself with the new fancy shower gel she was after buying, make up and then the dress. She was going to wear a red and black jersey dress over tights and dressy shoe boots that she had bought. Margaret had assured her that the dress highlighted her figure but had the allure of allowing a man that was interested to imagine what was underneath. It was casual enough as well not to look like she had overdone it. The shoe boots gave her a lift and highlighted her beautifully sculpted legs which were encased in sheer black tights. She reckoned if he had any interest then she should make an impression. She had spent a fortune on her elegant but casual look, so she hoped it would be worth it, and if not anyways hadn't she got a nice dress and boots in the strength of him. She had to remind herself again what the goal of the evening was. For her it was to get to know him a bit better and see if there was any potential for a relationship. She already knew that the answer from her side was a resounding yes, but she needed to establish if it was mutual. If there was some potential, then she would try and get another date. This could be a walk or cycle or something active where they would be both in their comfort zone, especially having viewed his Facebook page, which she must be careful not to mention to him or he might think she was some sort of a stalker. But she reassured herself that it was okay to look him up because everyone did it nowadays.

As she sprinted out the door to make sure she got there on time she wondered what his time keeping would be like. She had inherited the early gene from both her parents and being on time was important to her. In this case she aimed to be just on time although naturally that would include waiting the 5 minutes in the carpark because she would unquestionably be there for five to seven just in case. As she pulled into the carpark, she saw him striding out the other exit towards the restaurant. Wow, he looked amazing in converse, black jeans, blue jacket and black shirt. He moved with a natural inbuilt ease of movement that many athletes have. She gave him a few minutes before following him into the restaurant, right on the dot of 7pm. He was sitting down at the table chatting to the waitress when she arrived, and as soon as he saw her, he smiled that megawatt smile and lifted his hand to greet her. As she slid into the seat opposite him, he said, "Glad to see you are a good time keeper and didn't keep me waiting. By the way I must say you dry out well." She laughed and said, "Right back at you, looks like neither of us got pneumonia anyways after our drenching."

There was a little awkward silence for a few seconds and then they settled into some general small talk, while perusing the menu. She asked, "Have you been out since Sunday?" and he said, "No, I am mainly only a weekend cyclist these days. How about you?" She replied that she had been out Wednesday evening for a short one as it was her primary source of exercise at the moment. They circled each other in general conversation for a while. Saoirse thought this is not going too great we need to change the topic a little bit, so she asked, once their order had been taken, "tell me a bit about you." He said "I am not really that interesting. What is it you want to know?" "Well, I already know you're a cyclist, that you work in technology, you're from South Kerry, how about you tell me what makes you tick, what movies, books, music, food or sport you are into? How many in your family? Are you in a relationship? I don't know what do people who don't know each other generally talk about?" "Christ that makes this sound like an interview and here was I thinking we were just out for a casual bit of grub … I will tell you what we will do," he continues, "we will trade, I will tell you one thing about me in exchange for one piece of information about you. How does that sound?" "You're on, that's a deal, but you first since I asked first." "Let's take books," he begins, "I like to read autobiographies of sports people, real life stories of those who have achieved in their field. I find them fascinating and motivational. It doesn't have to be any particular sport, I am not fussy and I would read about any athlete because it's their mind set that really interests me. They are mostly so driven and put hours of training as well as having natural ability into their chosen sport be it running, cycling, climbing, football. They eat, live, breathe and sleep it. That's enough about me now, I could probably talk about this all night, what about you? What books are you into? Maybe you don't read." "Okay" she begins, "I also like to read but I am more into fiction although I have read some of the sports books as well and I know what you mean about their mind-sets." "What kind of fiction are you into?" "To be honest it really depends on what is going on in my life and how I am feeling when I pick up the book if I buy it. It can be historical fiction, romance, thrillers, bestsellers, social commentary, to be honest I am not fussy and I will read anything especially if I get it for free from someone else. I don't like the really gory thrillers though, as I am not into violence and especially not sexual violence. Where I am concerned the same goes for movies and TV. I better shut up on this topic for now because if I get started I will be on my soapbox for the night and bore you brainless." "Well" he said "to some level I agree with you on this but I do like a good action movie."

At that point the food arrived. She had ordered chicken fajitas which she was a big fan of when she was out because she never really could get them just right at home. He had roast beef with potatoes and vegetables and told her his preference is for the traditional plain food rather than the fancy stuff, although he would eat that too. As the meal progressed and they got to know each other better they really seemed to be getting along quite well. Once mains were finished Saoirse decided to go to the toilet for a break to freshen up and because she needed to go anyways. Left to his own devices Donal allowed himself time to muse on the dinner so far. She was good company; they were getting on well and she had a killer body in that dress. He wouldn't mind investigating what was under it. He thought at one stage that he had caught a glimpse of a beautiful pert breast encased in a black silk bra when she bent over and he wondered what she had matching it down below. A woman like her would definitely be matching, he thought to himself. He had to give himself a shake and remind himself that he had sworn off women for good. There was no way he was going back there, especially not with this one, he had seen her with her claws out after all, even if it was only for a short while. He had to admit though, who was he codding? There was something about her or he wouldn't be here otherwise. In all fairness this 'thank you' dinner really was a date just with another name and he had agreed to come. He was no fool, anyone could see that.

It had been such a long time since he was with a woman that he had practically become a monk, and he was only 32 years old. He decided, for Saoirse he could break his self-imposed promise of celibacy. There wouldn't be any harm in it, and Saoirse was certainly sending out the signals.

He would just relax and see where the evening went. He got the distinct feeling from her that she was interested in him but he wasn't too sure if she would be up for sex with no strings attached. He really didn't want to insult her, but he wasn't prepared to get involved in anything else. Or was he? She seemed more like the long-term relationship type. In his gut he felt Saoirse was a one man-woman, she seemed genuine and he would bet on it that she would be faithful to whomever she was in a relationship with. Although hadn't he also thought that about his ex? Whom he thought was mad about him, and look where that got him? He had nearly bought the ring for Christ's sake! What a fool he had been. Yes, for now at least, the only thing he was interested in from any woman was 'sex' or 'friendship' but not a relationship.

Saoirse came back smelling wonderful after having a squirt of something, and he thought to himself, she is definitely interested alright! Donal man you still have it, he thought to himself. They both ordered desert, apple tart and cream for Donal and chocolate fudge cake for Saoirse, although she wasn't too sure where she was going to put it after the fajitas. She could sense a mood shift in him since returning from the toilet, and she was wondering what he had been brooding about. She had seen the scowl on his face as she came back to the table which he shook off once he saw her, but the mood lingered. The rest of the meal went well; they were easy in each other's company. They seemed to be into the same things and the conversation just flowed from topic to topic. She looked at her watch and realised that it was nearly 10pm, they had been chatting for 3 hours. Time had absolutely flown by. Handing him a card with her number on it jokingly she said "for the next time, right now I had better get going as I have an early start tomorrow morning." She paid up and he walked her to her car.

On reaching the car she said, "you have my number, I am not going to beat around the bush with you, I really enjoyed this evening and I would love to see you again, call me." He said, "I also had a really good time too but look I am not really looking for anything right now, I am sorry if I gave you another impression, it's a long story." As her face dropped, he tried to soften it a bit, but probably only made it worse, by saying "Maybe if you are around some weekend we could go for a cycle or something, no strings. I will give you a text if I am heading out." Totally deflated she said "fine see you around" and jumped into her car and waved at him. Once he left, she put her head down on the steering wheel and cried her eyes out: "The fucker and his no strings." She had felt that the evening had gone really well up until that point. What was wrong with her, why does she always have to pick the unavailable, complicated ones? Why couldn't it be easy for her like her friends, they just seem to find guys and it all works out for them. She had really liked him and felt that there was a mutual spark there, and for once she didn't think it was her imagination reading too much into a situation. After all, hadn't they been flirting and talking for three hours and it only seemed like they had been there about an hour. Margaret was right after all, yet again she had built it up only to end in disappointment. When was she going to learn?

As Donal walked back to his car he felt like a right shit. He saw the disappointment in her eyes and it was not even like he was not attracted to her. If things had been different, he would have been the one looking for another date and he had to hand it to her, she had the guts to ask him straight out. He had also felt the chemistry and sexual tension between them. Why couldn't he have kissed her goodbye in the car park and made an arrangement to meet again? I mean, a cycling trip with no strings attached! How insulting was that? It was worse than offering a night of mad sex with no strings attached. To make himself feel better he rationalised that at least he was honest and she seemed like a girl who appreciated honesty rather than games. Christ, he acknowledged that despite all the counselling, he was still in a right mess because of the break-up. This evening had him questioning if the counselling had paid off at all. Then he reassured himself that he was able to go for the dinner and act normal enough around a woman, and that she actually wanted to see him again. That had to be progress from where he was this time last year.

CHAPTER 5

Life is a journey, with many twists; through each turn we learn something about ourselves

Saoirse woke up feeling groggy Friday morning, with a pounding headache and in a really bad mood. She decided to pull a sickie. She had never done it before, but she felt that she just couldn't face work, especially after she had told them all about meeting Donal and the impending date. Let them think that she had such a great night that she was just in no shape to come in. She just could not face the questions and the recounting that would have to be done. She felt like a total fool having yet again blown something out of all proportions with too high expectations. Her mind made up, she made the phone call to head office to confirm that she was taking a sick day. With that done she decided to have a duvet day and spend it in bed and wallow a little. She would read for a while, but mostly sleep; anyways she was wrecked as she hadn't slept much last night replaying the whole evening image by image like a slide show on a loop in her head.

She wished she was like some of her other friends who could moan to their mothers and get some sympathy. In her case, she knew that was wishful thinking, it was never going to happen. At times like this she really wished that herself and her mother got on better. Her co-workers and even her clients often talked about how they could tell their mothers anything, but that had never been true for her. Sometimes all a girl needed was a hug from her mother, to reassure her that everything would be alright. Her poor dad had always tried his best to make up for her mother, but good as he was, it just wasn't the same.

She pulled the duvet up over her head and after a good self-pitying cry, went back to sleep. On waking up a few hours later she had a look at her phone and there were a couple of texts enquiring after her wellbeing and how the date went. She just deleted them all as she couldn't be bothered dealing with them. She felt like such a fool. She had built this up to be her own personal fairy tale despite knowing better. As she got to the end of the messages, she noticed that there was one from Donal and her heart skipped a beat. It read, *"Sorry bout d end 2 last nite, I would like 2 c u again, how about that cycle Sat."* She got out of bed and decided to have a cup of tea to think about it, what was she going to do? Yes! she liked him. Yes! there seemed to be potential there. But! He was sending mixed messages. Yes! They had got on really well up until the end of last night. But what now? What did this text mean? In what context did he want to meet her again? Was this just another no strings cycle or was he offering more? She had a pain in her head thinking about it. She wondered would she ring Oisin to get his perspective as a male who regularly played the dating game? What she did know was she was not interested in another no strings male friendship, so Donal had better be offering something more than that. Giving herself a good mental shake she said to herself, I will not ring Oisin, I will make my own mind up. I will go for that cycle and see what is on offer and make a decision, but I will not be messed around by someone blowing hot and cold. She was also curious about the long story part and wondered what skeletons Donal had in the closet. She knew she hadn't imagined the sexual chemistry during the meal and she had not imagined his interest either. What she couldn't figure out was the abrupt rebuff at the end of the night. She was not however going to start second guessing herself for no man. She decided that she would meet him for the cycle but that she wasn't going to text him back until this evening, so she didn't come across as too keen. Having waited until the evening she replied *"apology accepted, where r we going? Where will I meet u?"* to which he replied, *"Muckross house, lets do Muckross n Dinish n Loughquitane n I'll treat u 2 coffee afterwards"* and she replied *"fine but only if d coffee includes cake. What time?"; "it can, how bout 10 am"; "right see u then"; "looking forward 2 it."*

Donal felt that this was a massive step forward for him. She had agreed to meet him again. He decided that he was not going to play any games with Saoirse, she was too nice a person to mess around and he really liked her based on their two previous encounters. He made up his mind that he was going to tell her a bit of his story to explain why he had cut her off so abruptly at the end of the previous night and if she could accept that then they could hopefully take it slowly from there. He was glad he had taken the initiative here because he supposed at some point he was going to have to get back on the horse again, unless of course he was going to embrace celibacy and resign himself to the life of a lonely bachelor having the odd meaningless sexual encounter to satisfy his baser needs. On a deeper level he knew that was not for him, although he was still not ready for a full-blown relationship. Then again, maybe Saoirse wasn't either and he was just blowing things out of proportion.

Saoirse had only put the phone down when it beeped again. God, she thought to herself, but he is a real eager beaver today. Wouldn't you think he would lay off it now that we have confirmed a date but when she looked at the phone, the message was from Oisin and it read "*Hi S u around for d wkend? Want 2 hit d road sat*" bloody hell she thought, that's two offers in the space of half an hour and she had been considering a weekend of feeling sorry for herself and wallowing in self-pity. She replied *"around alright but have date with another man and bike sat."* To which he replied, "*Who is he? tell all.*" She responded, *"can't early days."*

Oisin was taken aback, never before had Saoirse given him the brush off. He had just taken it for granted that she would be around and willing to go for a day out with him whenever he was available. He began to wonder who this fella that Saoirse was after meeting was and how serious was it. Obviously, he is another cyclist, but how long have they been seeing each other. It amazed him that she hadn't mentioned anything the last time he saw her, but that was two or three weeks ago and he had spent most of that time rambling on about the girl from Galway from the hen. I never even asked her about her love life, he thought. Now that I think about it, I rarely ever ask her about her love life. We always discuss mine but never hers. I just assumed that she rarely sees anyone because she is mostly available whenever I am. I hope this dick-head knows how lucky he is and will treat her right. He would hate to see her hurt by anyone. Saoirse had been his best friend for the past three years, even though they had known each other longer. When he had the car crash and was badly battered, she was the one who visited him in the hospital and called out to the house regularly to cheer him up. It's at a time like that that you realise who your real friends are. So many others had promised to visit but had never arrived; she however had made the time for him. He would give her a text later in the week to see if she would be around for a walk or a short cycle, some evening after work. He could find out about your man then.

Saoirse and Donal met in Muckross on Saturday morning as planned. They decided to head off for the cycle first and go for a cup of tea and a tasty cake afterwards. It was another beautiful morning and again the scenery was majestic, as they headed out around the circle route between Muckross and Dinish. The light flickering through the trees and the glimmer of the lake here and there as they passed. Between the beautiful scenery and negotiating the early morning walkers this leg of the journey was quite leisurely. It didn't however give them much opportunity to chat as the road was narrow and rough, so they mostly had to cycle in single file. Conversation although sporadic this morning, was easy, light, and friendly, and with no mention of their parting on Thursday night. Saoirse had decided that as he had invited her, he was going to have to bring it up himself. She was not going to help him on that count. It was bad enough to be mortified the last evening without going back for a second helping of humiliation. They stopped at the first bridge as is the custom to look out over the lake on both sides. To the right you can see the Hotel Europe out across the expanse of water and to the left you have the tree lined slopes of Torc mountain, straight ahead and slightly to the right is Tomies mountain and Tomies wood, another regular walking spot and now the home to some eagles. Close to the bridge Saoirse noticed that the base of her tree was not submerged in water today which told her that the water level in the lake was low. She has often wondered how this particular tree survives and doesn't rot but as long as she can remember that tree has been living both in and out of the water.

On the bridge Donal turned to Saoirse and taking her two hands in his said, "Look, I am really sorry about how I ended the night on Thursday. I know you were disappointed but it's a long story." She was enjoying her morning out and didn't really want to face this discussion just yet. She replied, "Let's just forget it for now and maybe come back to it over coffee and enjoy the morning." Leaning over he placed a whisper of a kiss on her lips that had the promise of so much more. Letting go of her hand he continued, "All right so, but I do need to talk to you about it." Wow she thought as she jumped back on her bike, I wouldn't mind some more of that.

As they passed Dinish cottage they noticed that there were already a few in there for tea, and others outside on the picnic benches enjoying the breathtaking view. The cottage itself is a beautiful old hunting lodge which has been renovated. If you look closely at the glass on window panes you can see where lovers and travellers as far back as the mid 1800s have inscribed their names and love notes on the glass. It can be an interesting read over coffee if you are lucky enough to get one of the window tables. When walking this particular route, the coffee shop is one of Saoirse's regular pit stops, as the cake is exceptional, and the stop is about half way around the lake for those on foot. Behind the cafe is the meeting of the waters where the lakes and the river collide from three different directions with the backdrop of the old weir bridge and an overhang of trees. On a fine day Saoirse could just sit here all day and let the world go by. It is a truly peaceful spot when undisturbed by other humans and on a busy day a good vantage point to watch the tourist boats that travel the lake and river between Ross Castles and Lord Brandon's Cottage on their way to the Gap of Dunloe.

Once on the main road, they take a left, pick up the speed and head back towards Killarney riding alongside the lake. It is nice for a change to be doing this section of the road with fresh legs because normally this is the section that kills Saoirse, as it's usually at the end of a long cycle. In her mind she is back in Killarney but in reality, there are a couple of miles of low grade climbing and steady pulls, nothing terribly challenging, but on tired legs they can be tough. On fresh legs and with someone to slipstream, it's a dawdle. Heading out the Cork road for Glenflesk they get their first opportunity to really chat as they can cycle as a pair on the hard shoulder.

Donal decides this is his opportunity to have the conversation because he won't have to face her directly when they are on their bikes. If she gets mad, she can always let the steam off on the hill on the way up from Glenflesk to Loughguittane and she more than likely will have cooled off by the time they head for tea. He had come to the conclusion that while she was hot tempered, she wasn't the type to hold a grudge, so it was better to just get this out of the way. He decided nothing like taking the 'bull by the horns' so to speak and spit it out. "Saoirse, I know we said we would wait until coffee for this conversation, but I just want to get it off my chest." He was nervous so it came out all wrong. "Look Saoirse, you really are a grand girl, and I like you, but at the moment I am not really looking for a relationship." That drove her mad immediately. A "grand girl"! For God's sake, what era was he from? she fumed to herself. It sounded like he could be her grandfather. "God all mighty Donal" she spat out "aren't you getting a bit ahead of yourself here. Who said anything about a relationship we have only met three times so far and one of them was by chance."

Nothing for it now he decides but explain the whole story or he worried she would consider him a complete nut case. So, he carried on "Before you bite the head off me, I just wanted to be honest with you in case you are expecting anything more from me. You see I got badly hurt before, in that I found out my girlfriend had been cheating on me, around the same time as I was planning to propose to her. For that reason, I had made up my mind to steer clear of women altogether, that was until I met you." Looking over at him she could see the pain in his face and reaching out she touched his arm as they were cycling along. "I am sorry to hear that," she responded. Taking a breath he carried on "Saoirse I like being with you, I would like to get to know you better, but I don't know if I can offer you what you are looking for." As he was rambling on Saoirse was thinking to herself Jesus, I do pick them, but, she said to him. "Look Donal, I appreciate you telling me that, it can't have been easy and I am really sorry that your ex ruined your faith in women, but you know we are not all like that." "Yes I know that but I think I would find it really hard to trust someone else again, I know this is a lot to land on you and we hardly know each other but I have to be honest" he replied. "Look there is no pressure here. I think you are a really nice guy. I enjoy your company and I think we have some chemistry between us unless I am mistaken but it's early days. I would be happy to take it slow if you are interested and just go on the journey and see where the road takes us so to speak."

They passed the rest of the cycle without incident and realised that they were a well-matched pair on the bikes. Both were quite powerful on the hills although Donal was much stronger on the flat but decided to take it handy so they could chat. Over tea and cake, they decided that they would meet again and maybe go for a drink on Thursday night.

Monday after work Saoirse decided to call into Margaret and give her the update. She was still unsure of Donal, while she was attracted to him, and the kiss on the bridge held some promise, the way he blurted out the story of his ex was really quite strange. She was wondering if he was so scarred from that experience that he might be emotionally unstable. It was the clumsiest way of building a relationship that she had ever experienced although she acknowledged she didn't have too much experience of it. She had to hand it to him: He was at least honest and wasn't trying to hide behind any bravado. For a gorgeous, tough-looking guy, he was soft with a caring streak and she felt there was some chemistry between them. However, his experience with his ex was still hanging over him and she certainly didn't want to be his rebound relationship.

After giving Margaret the run down she inquired, "so what do you think?" Margaret in her no nonsense way said, "I can't tell you what to do, you have to decide for yourself, but in the past I always asked myself some questions; Am I attracted to him?; Does meeting him excite me?; Can I trust him?; If things progressed could I imagine waking up next to him every morning? If you can honestly answer 'yes' to all of them then I think you should give him a chance and see if ye have something between ye. It sounds like it might be a bit of hard work, but no relationship is plain sailing, they all have their up and downs." From where Saoirse stood right now, she could definitively say

'Yes' she was attracted to him, he was gorgeous; 'Yes' he excited her, she had felt the fizz right from the start, even in the pouring rain under the trees stranded on the side of the road. The brief kiss on the bridge had been exquisite and she could imagine that he would be really good in bed. Despite his insecurities over his ex, he had an innate, virile masculinity, yet was considerate and caring. She imagined he would be into energetic, shared and pleasurable love making. She didn't know him well enough to know if she could trust him or not, but he seemed like the honest type so that probably would be yes. As for waking up next to him every morning, that was a bit far down the road. For now, she would settle with waking up next to him the odd morning - so, to be fair to herself, she could probably say that the answer to most of the questions was yes.

She hadn't realised that she was pacing and debating with herself in her head until Margaret said "earth to Saoirse anything going on in there" at which point she jumped and replied, "you know what I think I will give it a go with him." She had no sooner uttered the words when her phone pinged and she saw his name come up on a text: *"Hi really enjoyed d cycle, but can't make Thursday, How about d Gap on Saturday instead"* without thinking she replied, *"Sure only if we do dinner afterwards in Kate's."*

Oisin was sitting at home recovering from the weekend when he decided to call over to Saoirse for a cup of tea and a bit of a chat. He was in the car backing out the drive when he suddenly thought, shit I had better text her in case your man is over with her. He didn't want to walk in on the two of them cosying up for the evening so he sent her a text *"Hi S u at home this evening"* and got one back straight away saying *"no out and about, but will be in tomorrow if u want 2 catch up." "Grand so, c u 2morrow"* he sent back. He got out of the car feeling a bit deflated and finding himself at a bit of a loose end wondering what he would do with himself now. He wasn't used to Saoirse not being around when he wanted to drop in, it was so strange she had always been there in the past whenever he was available. He just took it for granted that he was the one with the social life and other than her physical activity and the odd night out with the girls she was usually available. He was telling himself that it was no big deal. Sure, he had loads of friends; he would just call over to the lads instead. But he could feel himself a bit irritated and, truth be told, he could feel a sort of hollowness in his gut. The only contact he had had with Saoirse in the last few weeks was in response to his text to her. Thinking about it, she hadn't picked up the phone once to text him or arrange to meet up which was most unlike her. This relationship with the 'your man' must be getting serious, however he rationalised that he and Saoirse were only friends, so she was entitled to get on with her own life.

Tuesday evening and Oisin arrived with his customary pack of purple Snacks for the tea. This was their usual, whenever he called over. His mother had taught him from a young age; you couldn't go calling to someone with your hands hanging. You had to bring something for the tea. As he was pulling into the door in his new red Audi, or the passion wagon as he liked to call it, he felt a bit strange. He was now the other man in Saoirse's life. Yes, she had been with guys previously, but this seemed a bit more serious.

Saoirse had been his best buddy for the past few years; he had shared all of his ups and downs with her, including the numerous tales of his weekend conquests. He had seen her in all her states, from worn out, dog tired after a gruelling day out on the bike to being dressed to kill at some of the weddings that they went to together. Ah, he thought, up to now he could always rely on Saoirse to be his plus one at a wedding. She was always so charming, and she understood clearly that they were just friends, unlike other women he had gone to events with as a plus one. They were always trying to make something more out of it. Some of his friends would joke about the fact that they were like an old, married couple; they knew each other so well. It was nearly a given at this stage that you could almost put Oisin and Saoirse on the invite. They both enjoyed each other's company and that was as far as it went a modern platonic friendship. Now he supposed all of that was about to change with this new guy on the scene.

In the past few weeks, he couldn't put his finger on it, but something was eating at him and he was off form. Even his brother Mike had commented yesterday, "What's eating you man? You're not a bit like yourself lately?" And Mike, bless him, wouldn't be the most sensitive or observant. Oisin reflected that, if he had noticed he must be away off. Usually a happy go lucky easy-going sort of fellow he found himself irritable and he couldn't quiet make out what was wrong with him. Here again, walking up to her door he could feel the irritation. It annoyed him; that for the first time ever he actually had to make an arrangement to call over to Saoirse. Thinking about it he supposed that was only fair as she never really just waltzed in his door unannounced. As he walked up to her door, past the beautiful manicured borders of her lawn, he thought to himself she really has done a good job on this place. He remembered when she was buying it and she had taken him to have a look at it to see what he thought. It was a wreck with a hole in the roof and the rain pouring through. The garden had been completely overgrown. It bore no resemblance to the cottage garden it had once been. It had totally reverted to what nature had intended in this part of the boggy Irish countryside. It was full of rushes, furze bushes and sally trees.

Now it was as pristine as Saoirse herself. Although he had to admit she was no stranger to hard work. She had put in many back-breaking hours into the house in order to achieve the amazing results now on display. She had done most of the planting and hedging herself, with him and her father pitching in the odd weekend to give her a hand with the heavy lifting. It was backbreaking removing the trees, and there were also plenty of stones to be picked in the lawn before it could be turned back into grass. He admitted she had truly transformed the place in such a short space of time.

Pressing the doorbell he waited for her to answer instead of his usual knock and walk in. She answered the door in her ponytail, leggings and loose dancers top that she favoured when relaxing at home. It was like he had received a kick in the gut, it just hit him. He knew instantly what was wrong with him. It had been right there in front of him all along. Saoirse was standing there in the evening sunlight saying, "Why are you ringing the doorbell, wasn't I expecting you?" She joked, "This makes a change; you usually just waltz in here like you own the place. Are you feeling alright? Why are you ringing the door-bell like a stranger and texting before you come over?" While she was ranting away, he was just staring at her, she was really stunning with those beautiful deep brown eyes and perfect skin; smiling, bubbly and energetic. He felt his stomach contract; she was his friend, but right now he knew he wanted so much more.

It took all his self-control to resist the urge to pull her into his arms and kiss her senseless at that moment. Am

I going crazy? he wondered. He felt totally thrown off balance by the depth of this sudden attraction. How could this be happening, this was Saoirse he reasoned to himself, the woman he had spent so many comfortable hours with; cycling, walking, having tea and never once had he desired her and certainly not like this. OK, he always knew she was a fine looking woman, hadn't the lads and even his mother pointed that out to him. His mother, bless her, could never understand what he was doing chasing around after all them 'flighty things', when he had such a fine woman in Saoirse if he just opened his eyes. "Oh Mom" he said in silence, "you wouldn't believe this, but my eyes are now open wide, but maybe it's too late." This was the real deal, his heart was pumping, blood pounding in his head. What the hell was wrong with him, it's not like he ever had problems around women before but then he thought, "yeah but it never mattered and she was never my best friend, who is now seeing someone else." Like some involuntary movement that he had no control over, he saw his hand reach out to touch her. The urge was so strong, to feel the soft sleekness of her hair, but luckily for him at that moment she stepped back from the door and said "come on in will you before I catch my death" and went into the kitchen. He had no choice but to follow her and luckily for him, it broke the trance he was in and gave him a few moments to gather himself.

He followed her into the kitchen taking in her beautiful athletic body, while wondering why he had never noticed her as a woman before. She had the most beautiful, long, slender, yet strongly muscled legs, that stretched up from dainty ankles to a fine, pert-toned backside and up to that beautiful long graceful neck. He was in a complete daze and was following her in silence which was totally unlike him. Usually by this stage, he would have launched into some tale. Instead he was just dumbstruck, he realised what a fool he had been, here she was right under his nose all this time and he had never really seen her, he just took her for granted as his friend. He was utterly floored.

After switching on the kettle, she turned to him and said "Oisin, I think I might be in love," and his heart just leaped in his chest. For one fabulous instant he thought she must be a mind reader. In his head, he was crying out; me too Saoirse, me too, but if only you knew it. Jokingly he said, "I know isn't it amazing that it took you so long, and you nearly over the hill at 30." This was a long running joke between the two of them, he remembered their pact clearly. They had made it after some wedding they had attended. They had agreed that if they both reached 35 and were still single, they would get married to prevent them going into old age alone. "I know what you mean like, I am 29 years old and will be 30 after the Ring this year, maybe this is it" she said wistfully. "Maybe Donal is the one. I must tell you all about him" and she launched into tales of how amazing Donal was. As Oisin was sitting there, his heart was sinking. Shit he said to himself, I have really messed up here. The love of my life is about to slip through my fingers in the same instant I realise what she means to me. He knew she hadn't the slightest clue of how he was feeling, after all hadn't he gone out of his way over the years to point out what a good friendship they had. What a laugh all that was now, all that stuff he had rattled on about, about two members of the opposite sex just being friends. Who had I been kidding all along? he thought to himself. He knew it was true for some, but in this case, it was a total myth. For now, he made up his mind to play it cool and he might still be in with a chance, but one thing was for certain, he wasn't going to give her up without a fight. Right then and there he decided to hang in there no matter how hard it was. He would let this relationship of hers run its course and be there to pick up the pieces when she needed him. After all, she didn't have much of a track record with men, she usually managed to scare away anyone who attempted to stick around all by herself.

Once the tea was over, he decided that, to give her some space to think, he would head off home, even though it was much earlier than his usual departure. To soften it and keep his leg in, he said, "Saoirse how would you feel about doing our annual test cycle on the Gap on Saturday?" "Sorry Ois, no can do as I have something else on," she replied. She didn't elaborate and he didn't ask for specifics but assumed correctly that he was getting blown off so she could spend time with Donal. He decided then and there that 'in for a penny, in for a pound' and an intervention would need to happen sooner than he thought if he was to be in with a real chance with her. Taking a deep breath, he said "You know the way my lease is up at the end of the month, is there any chance that I could use your spare room for a few weeks. It would be just until I find someone else to share with. I will pay rent and half the bills and everything. I know you like your space and that you vowed never to house share again after your last experience, but is there any chance of it?" Saoirse was taken aback with this request, as, although they had been really good friends, they had never lived in each others pockets and with Oisin being a lads 'lad' and into his women, she was wondering if her cottage wasn't going to be a bit small and rural for him. It certainly wouldn't be much of a bachelor pad, with her wandering around the place. Saoirse said "Sure if you are stuck you can move in for a few weeks until you find something, but I can't take money for it, after all you practically renovated the place for me." Nearly choking he said, "Sure what are friends for if we can't help each other out?" "When were you actually thinking about moving in?" she asked. "Well as I said, we have to be out of our gaff by the end of the month and that's next Monday, so I suppose early Sunday unless you have any objections." Damn Saoirse thought to herself, I was planning on inviting Donal back here on Saturday night. She had it all planned out, a day cycling, dinner and a few drinks in Kate Kearney's and then back to her place to see where the evening would take them. She had hoped to investigate if there was any passion behind the chemistry she felt. In her own head she had already imagined them easing out each others kinks after a day's cycling followed by some fabulous sex on her beautiful Egyptian cotton sheets, which were freshly laundered and ready to go on the bed Saturday morning. Sunday morning had been formed in her head, they would be having a long lazy day in bed making glorious love, followed by a leisurely breakfast in her new silk dressing gown. She had even gone out and bought some new special matching underwear also for the occasion. All the preparations were in place, she had it all worked out in her head and of course she reckoned that Donal would go along with it.

Now with Oisin's bombshell none of this could be a reality, nothing like some fella hauling in boxes and banging around the place to break the magic. She could feel the colour of embarrassment and annoyance creeping up her neck but she was unable to go back on her promise to her good friend, even if it meant not being able to put her fantasy into action. She guessed that she wouldn't be having Donal over for a bit longer, until she got used to the idea of having Oisin living here and the two of them had met. Oisin felt a little bad because he could see that he had ruined her plans, but ever the lady, she would not let him out on the streets and he had counted on that. After all, as the saying goes "all's fair in love and war" and he knew now that he was prepared to go to war for Saoirse. He would do whatever it took.

CHAPTER 6

Calm water is a balm to the turbulent soul

Having put his intervention in place, Oisin decided that he needed to plan out a strategy. This was all a bit spur of the moment, which despite his general blasé appearance, that was not how he operated at all. He decided to go for a walk down the copper mines trail near Ross Castle and sit for a while in his favourite spot. Some might call it practicing mindfulness as was the current fashion, but he was coming here to sort his thoughts, long before that had become a fad. It was a little bit of a walk to get there but well worth the effort. He usually went around in front of the Castle and down the trail by the boat house. He did this because he liked this rougher trail more than the tarred road. He followed the meander of the mud path under the trees, which in spring is home to beautiful clusters of wild bluebells but tonight, he could smell the wild garlic. He loved the simple wilderness of it, particularly as it was accessible and so close to the town. One minute you could be in your car driving through traffic and the next you have plenty of space to breathe and think. Once he emerged from the path, he took the road past the beautiful vistas of the lake with Torc mountain in the background. Mangerton and its punch bowl lay further afield. However, his favourite place was down a small, secluded path from the road with a rocky beach at the end that had a big slab of stone. It just welcomed a backside and a troubled head. Here he could sit and gaze out across the lake, with no one to bother him. The water lapping on the shore, birds twittering in the trees and the hum of an outboard engine of an angler's boat out on the lake were the only sounds to accompany his thoughts.

Sitting down and taking in a deep breath of the fresh unpolluted air he let his thoughts wander. He really couldn't believe that she had been right there under his nose all along. He realised that it was not until he was threatened with losing her that he realised how strong his feelings for Saoirse were. Ever since he had first met Saoirse, he acknowledged that he was always drawn to her. He always enjoyed being in her company, but never in a romantic sort of way. Listening to her talking about Donal this evening was like a knife being twisted in his gut. This was all completely new to him. No one up to this point had ever taken up this sort of space in his head or heart before and he reckoned he was in for a rough ride. This was totally uncharted territory for him. Could he really go through with living with her? Could he bear seeing Donal around her, listen to their stories, see them cozying up together or, worse, getting up in the morning and seeing him in the kitchen knowing where he had slept the previous night? It was time for him to answer a few serious questions. Would he really be able to bide his time and see her with Donal or would that crush him? He was unsure, but even at the thought of Donal, he felt a tightening in his chest. How would he be if she had him over and they were sleeping together in the next room? Could he really handle it or had he been way too hasty with his decision to move in. Maybe he would be better off keeping to the background until this relationship blew over. If he were to truthfully examine his conscience, could he really actively sabotage her relationship with Donal? If he did and she found out Saoirse certainly wouldn't thank him for it. He was now stuck between the proverbial 'rock and a hard place' and he had no choice but to wait it out and see how things would progress. He would have to sleep on his decision to move in, because he was not too sure if he actually could handle his feelings for her at such close quarters. He acknowledged that even if Donal was out of the picture, he would now have some job to try and convince her to see him as more than a friend. He figured he wasn't going to resolve this one in one go, so he decided to set it aside and just enjoy the solitude of the lake for a while.

After a fitful night's sleep with some crazy dreams he came to the conclusion that he just couldn't do it to himself. He couldn't be in the same house and watch them romancing, while his heart was breaking. Before he could change his mind and ponder any more on the subject he pulled out his phone and sent a text to Saoirse *"Don't want 2 cramp ur style n ur love nest at d moment, I will move back n with Mom nd Dad for a few weeks until I find somewhere else."* He would have to find other ways to be around Saoirse and hope that her relationship with Donal wouldn't last. He just knew whatever happened he wouldn't be able to live with her under these circumstances.

Seeing the text Saoirse was torn. She replied, *"if ur sure, u know dere is always room for u here."* To tell the truth she had come to terms with him moving in and was actually looking forward to it. She knew it might have been a bit awkward with Donal, but she and Oisin had always got on so well, it would have been fun to have had him around. On another level though, Saoirse was relieved, starting a new relationship with a live-in house guest could have led to some embarrassing moments. It might have been a bit overcrowded if both Oisin and Donal were here, although she thought the lads would have got on well together, they were similar in many ways. She knew initially Oisin would have given Donal a thorough interrogation about his intentions as he had always been a bit protective of her with other fellows, but she was OK with that. She had just assumed that it was her best friend looking out for her and Margaret would do the same. Other lads though sometimes were intimidated by it.

Thinking about the text, what she couldn't understand was the sudden change of mind and why he was moving back in with his mother and father. He had vowed he would never do that as his mother would suffocate him in a well-meaning way. The dinner would be on the table and in exchange he would have to report on all the happenings in his life. It was only well-meaning interest, but it drove him mad. He preferred to be able to come and go as he pleased. He often said there is no such thing as privacy or a free lunch in that house.

Saoirse used to laugh about that because there was loads of space in the big, old rambling house and she loved his mother. She often joked with Oisin that his mother could make a meal out of thin air, no matter what time of the day or night someone showed up. But she did understand where Oisin was coming from. There was loads of space, but the family were a larger than life sort of gang. His mother had an open-door policy, and all his brothers and sisters were in and out of the house all of the time. No one ever made an arrangement to visit. They just arrived. They didn't live in each other's pockets, but they asked very personal questions without even thinking about them. Whether you asked for it or not, you got an opinion on everything from what you should wear, to who you should be seeing, to who will win the game on Sunday. While he loved his family dearly, he just didn't like living with them at 30 years of age, seeing them day in and day out. Oisin liked his space more than the rest of them, but Saoirse reckoned it was because as the youngest, the rest of his family thought they had a God given right to tell him what to do more so than anyone else in the household. He had often told her how much he loved the house, a big, old rambling farmhouse that had been built onto many times, but he had also vowed he would never move back in there unless he owned it himself. Although he loved his mother dearly, and it was obvious as her youngest he had a special place in her heart, he hated her telling him what to do. Saoirse chuckled to herself because for the past few years, Oisin's mother had been on a right old bandwagon about Oisin settling down and finding the right woman. All the rest of his siblings were married and as she had said many a time "if I could just sort you out my life's work would be done."

Saoirse laughed to herself again as she remembered the time Oisin's mother had even made a not so subtle suggestion that Oisin and herself would be a good match. She had actually said "What are ye doing fooling around with this 'friends' carry on? In my day if you went out a few times with a fellow you were considered doing a line and one thing led to another. You certainly wouldn't be going away with them for a weekend or a holiday and not be getting married after it." His mother could not understand the concept of a platonic relationship. But Saoirse acknowledged she was a mighty woman to organise a good party. Some of the best evenings Saoirse had were at Oisin's house, at his mother's summer garden parties as she liked to call them. Oisin was the youngest of six, so these affairs were lively events, where all his siblings and their broods attended, and the odd friend would be invited as well. She always got an invite and was quite fond of Oisin's mother despite her meddling around in their relationship. Thinking on it, she wondered would she get an invite this year now that she was seeing Donal. She assumed not. Generally, the party was about two weeks before the Ring of Kerry cycle. Most years, by the time the party rolled around she and Oisin would have spent many a happy Sunday out on their bikes together.

Saoirse assumed that his mother would be hopeful that her party might seal the deal between the two of them. The party would usually start with everyone heading out into the garden to have a game of Gaelic football, soccer or tag rugby. Teams would be made up of men, women and children. Pregnancy or injury was the only ticket out of the game. If it was a wet summer, after the game the lawn would look like a herd of cattle had been let out in it, but they took no notice. Games were energetically contested with everyone shouting at each other and making tackles as if they were in an All-Ireland final. The noise level would be spectacular, only the racket that a large family getting together can make. If it was really warm after the game, they would all go down to the river at the bottom of the field in front of the house for a swim to cool off before the food. The competition continued down there with a swimming gala where everyone was encouraged to give their best. No corner was given as they competed for family honour in each event. On return from the river his mother and father would have a barbeque with some of the best steaks and sausage, as well as a few salads all made from his mother's garden. There would be a small bit of drink to be sociable, although they were not really that much into the drink. It was more about everyone getting together and having the chat and a laugh. His mother loved having everyone under her roof and all together, even if it was for only one evening.

Once the small children were gone to bed his brother would pull out the guitar and there would be a sing song into the night. There were so many rooms in the house that they would all find somewhere to lie down and there wouldn't be too much fuss. Everyone would get up in the morning and there would be a massive fry-up where they would discuss their various injuries from the evening, before they went their separate ways. God she would miss them parties alright. Bringing her mind back to the present, she supposed it was Oisin's own choice to move back in home. She wondered how he would manage his love life now, because whatever about bringing his lady friends to her house, he certainly would not be bringing them to meet his mother. She decided that she would be generous, and she texted him "*well if u ever need a break from d folks, u know my door is always open.*" He replied "*thanks I might need to take you up on that from time to time*" keeping his options open and his leg in the door. In truth of course he had no intention of availing of her hospitality if Donal was shacking up with her.

CHAPTER 7

True friendship is like good wine; it develops and matures over time

Saturday arrived and Saoirse hopped out of bed and threw open the curtains to a morning haze that could only mean one thing, a rare scorcher of a day. Once the haze burned off it would be beautiful as forecasted; the temperatures set to rise up to the low 20s, which is high for Kerry in mid-May.

She instantly thought there is no way I am getting on a bike today. It will be too hot with the sun splitting the stones. Everyone was saying they hoped that this wasn't our summer, but she didn't care, she was going to make the most of it and she certainly would not spend this beautiful day on a bike. It was a day for the beach and nothing else. She would try out that new bikini she had bought; why keep it for a foreign holiday when she could be strutting her stuff on Rossbeigh beach and could get a fine colour into the bargain? She always believed that an Irish tan came half from the sun and half from windburn. Recently she heard some doctor on a morning radio chat show saying there was no such thing as windburn, it was just plain and simple sunburn. Who knew she thought when and if the health establishment would change their mind again on the matter. All she knew was that after a long, wet winter she was going to get to feel the sun on her body for the day and she couldn't wait.

No time for dawdling and wasting the day, she immediately sent a text to Donal *"fancy a change of plans? Body boarding at Rossbeigh."* As Oisin's father was fond of saying "you have to make hay while the sun shone" and as beach days were a rarity here, she had no intention of missing this one. She reckoned that Donal would look amazing on the beach. She could imagine him emerging from the water with his hair all wet and his top for body boarding moulded to his beautiful chest. He would be stunning. As her mind wandered in fantasy land, her phone pinged to announce a reply, but on seeing it her mood dropped *"Sorry! Sand nd salt water don't agree with me, d beach gives me rash, anyhow I thought we are training"* Damn thought Saoirse, she had been looking forward to spending the day with him. What was she going to do now? One thing was for sure, she was not going to sit at home and waste a fine day like this nor was she getting on a bike. She knew that if she went with him by the time she got to the Head of the Gap in this heat she would be as red as a tomato from head to toe with exertion and that certainly was not a good look if her seduction plans were to come to fruition. She replied *"u sure? days like these don't come around 2 often nd I would really like 2 go to the beach."* He replied *"why not head away yourself nd I will c u later, d beach really doesn't agree with me."* In a bit of a huff she replied *"u know what, I will, but I might not be around for dinner later depending on who I go with."* He replied *"no worries c u when I c u. Enjoy!"*

At this stage she was really annoyed, it was supposed to be a date, and who could not enjoy a day at the beach. Surely the rash couldn't be that bad. It was not like they got this weather every day. They could go cycling any day; in fact, they were both fit enough to do the Ring tomorrow if necessary. Her bubble was well and truly burst. Her fantasy had extended to them spending the day in romantic bliss, holding hands, walking along the beach, stopping for long kisses here and there, feeding each other their picnic, swimming in each others arms and riding the waves together followed by a lovely dinner in Glenbeigh or the Golden Nugget on the way home. Now all this was out the window, but the beach was calling her, and she had no intention of missing out. She would shelve her romantic plans for another day. After all he hadn't seemed too bothered if the tone of his text was anything to go by *"C u when I c u."* That didn't seem like someone too disappointed, did it?

Not one to be deterred easily once she got a notion into her head she sent a text to Oisin *"fancy a day n Rossbeigh"* only to get one back immediately *""must be a mind reader, boards already loaded."* At that she smiled to herself and thought, well at least I can depend on someone to be on the same page as me. *"Will you pick me up so?"* she replied. *"It's a date"* he responded. This stopped her in her tracks; it was a bit ironic to be going on 'a date' with her best friend rather than the man who was supposed to be her new boyfriend.

Thinking back, she remembered the many times in the early days of her friendship with Oisin that she had hoped for a response like this, but it never came. At the start she had often yearned for things between them to progress further than friendship, but it had never happened. Over time they had found a rhythm and a balance in their friendship. Now they were just good mates, but it was strange that he would call it 'a date'. It was most unlike him. He was the one always saying why can't two members of the opposite sex just be good friends. Giving herself a mental shake, she put these unsettling thoughts out of her head. That was all in the past now wasn't it, and she was generally happy with the way things were between them? He was a wonderful, reliable friend and she knew she could guarantee that she would have a good day out with him. They had a tried and tested routine developed over the years.

They would load everything up, body boards of course, the good ones that they bought in the outdoor shop. They had never quite progressed to surfing, they were happy to chase the waves with the boards. Wetsuits in case it was too cold and windy in Rossbeigh, no point getting back there and not being able to get in the water with the cold. It could be a wild spot and you never knew what it would be like until you got there.

Saoirse loved the wildness of the beach, on the side of the Atlantic Ocean with its rolling waves crashing in. The beach itself was testament to the power of the water. In one storm alone the end of the beach had become an island, as the storm waves had cut their own path through the sand dunes. Despite the wildness of the waves there was also a peace to be found there. She loved the fact that you could walk for miles along the beach, most of it in peace and quiet, away from other people as only the hardy souls ventured down to the end of the beach. Next in was the rash vest, for over her bikini in case it was warm enough not to use the wetsuit. Board rash was not a good look. She was prepared to overlook the farmer's tan in the pursuit of catching a few good waves, but she was not willing to deal with raw skin from board rash. She had learned that lesson the hard way many years ago and wasn't in any hurry to forget it. Once loaded they would drive to Glenbeigh, call into the filling station on the way for tuna rolls, packets of crisps and a bottle of fizzy drink for the picnic. She would forego healthy eating for one day, in her mind it was all part of the annual trip to the beach. Anyways she rationalised that they would do enough exercise to burn off whatever calories they consumed and more. A day at the beach with Oisin guaranteed you that. She figured if he was going to school these days, he would probably be labelled hyperactive. He always liked to be on the move and a day at the beach with him usually included walking, playing frisbee, beach soccer, body boarding, anything once he was moving.

Oisin wasn't into sunbathing at all; he always said that the best way to get a colour if you wanted was to be up and active but he preferred to look after his skin and always lathered on the sun screen. He always said you were better off out in the weather doing something productive rather than being thrown down on the ground turning yourself like a sausage in a frying pan. While she herself wasn't as fanatical when it came to sunbathing, she loved lying down under the cover of a book and people-watching.

Part of the fun of a day at a beach for her was speculating what the story was behind each group of people and what their relationships were like. She was interested in people generally. Once they got there they would park up and go for a walk along the back beach until they could get to the end before turning the corner to their picnic spot. A beautiful, secluded spot where only the brave walkers frequented was a fine hike, but oh so spectacular. Here they would have their picnic before heading back to the main beech to gather up their boards and gear to do battle with the waves. Enough of the day-dreaming and get ready or I will be late, Saoirse scolded herself, one of her own pet hates.

Just when she had thrown everything together the doorbell rang and in walked Oisin. He was looking well as he always did in his sandals, shorts, t-shirt and sunglasses pushed back on his head. He was a good dresser and she always liked that about him. He had a knack of getting the clothes just right for whatever the occasion; unlike so many other Irish men who God love them hadn't a clue when it came to clothes, unless their mothers, sisters, wives or girlfriends bought them and then practically dressed them. How many would they see today at the beach with their socks in sandals? She had to admit though the younger generation were more fashion-conscious and tended to take more pride in their appearance.

She looked at him and smiled, "Great day for the beach, is this all your gear here by the door? Will I throw it in the boot?" he asked. She shouted "yes please if you don't mind" as she dashed back down the corridor. "I'm just washing my teeth and I will be out in two minutes, to give you a hand." By the time she had given herself a last look at in the mirror, collected her wallet and washed her teeth, he had everything in the car. She closed and locked the door and jumped into the passenger seat. Pushing her sunglasses on she said, "Let's go and make a day of it, I am so excited that we finally got a fine day like this and that we are actually off work to enjoy it." Turning to him she asked, "Any news? You know I am actually surprised to see you today, I thought you would be packing." "Ah sure I saw the forecast yesterday and I knew today was going to be fabulous so I said, no way am I wasting the first beach day that I am off work, packing and moving … I asked Mike, the brother, to come over and give me a hand last night. I didn't have that much so we just gathered it all up and threw it into his van. I left it there and I will drag it in at home tomorrow. You wouldn't know how long this weather will last for and this could be the only day we get this summer, so we have got to make the most of it.

By the way to what do I owe the pleasure of your company to, I thought you would be off out with lover boy?" He couldn't quite bring himself to say Donal's name in her company, it was as if he said his name, it would make it real. A brief shadow crossed Saoirse's face and she said, "Apparently he is not into the beach as it gives him a rash or something. Anyway, he wants to get his training in." "Ouch" said Oisin "do I detect a hint of annoyance in that comment?" "To put it mildly 'yes' … but let's leave it go and enjoy our day together, it might be one of our last … I don't want to talk about it." At that remark Oisin felt the tightness in his stomach again and thought, "lover boy's loss and his first black mark against him."

He would certainly make the most out of their day. What sort of a fool was your man, passing up on the opportunity to spend the day with Saoirse in a bikini? Now that was a sight for sore eyes. What was your man thinking, in Oisin's opinion it would have been well worth a bit of rash but he decided to keep his own council on that matter. "Will we do the usual, the walk, the picnic and then the boarding?" he asked Saoirse. "I think some of the lads might be down as well, so I can play a game of soccer later while you toast yourself. What do you think?" "Sounds like a plan to me."

Saoirse was thinking we really are like an old married couple; I knew the drill before he ever picked me up. Having ordered the rolls and picked up the various bits and pieces for the picnic, on their way to pay he asked "do you want to throw yours up there with mine and I will pay for them?" "Ah no! I have cash myself and I can get them … if you start paying for things it might really seem like we are on a date." He laughed and says, "now wouldn't that be a turn up for the books." While he said it, she saw a tiny flicker of something that looked like pain pass across his eyes. She didn't comment but paid for her own and headed out to the car ahead of him. He came out with his picnic and two 99 ice-creams. He handed her one and she asked light-heartedly, "to what do I owe the pleasure of this?" He looked at her and said "It's nothing, I felt like one but I couldn't be gobbling down my own and you not having any." As she took the ice cream from him she thought that their fingers connected for a moment longer than necessary and she felt a little tingle of something, but she just shook it off and thought that she must be becoming a bit paranoid. Taking the first lick he said, "This is the life, what more could a man ask for freedom, good company and great ice-cream?"

CHAPTER 8

In life we have many choices each with its own set of consequences

On arriving at the beach, they drove in as far as they could along the stony carpark as there was no point having to drag everything too far. If the tide came in, the waves would be crashing up onto the rocks. They would have to keep backing up the beach ahead of it until you were on the rocks which don't make for comfortable sun loungers. From their parking spot they could easily drag their gear down to the section of beach just beyond the rocks which was safe from the incoming tide. Oisin liked to get to the beach early, to get one of these parking spots. Saoirse often teased him that he was a bit like the German tourists that would be down early to grab the sun loungers when holidaying abroad. With their parking spot secured, they could now head off on their walk and let the day heat up. They headed off along the back beach just shooting the breeze about this and that. The horses from the riding stables were out for a canter further along the beach. A few seagulls were swooping down into the water to their right and some children were running in and out of the dunes to their left. You could hear their laughs and calls to each other as they ran, sliding and jumping through the dunes. It was an ideal spot for children to play a game of hide and seek. There was one family setting up for a barbecue. The perfect location, as this stretch of the beach was sheltered from the winds by the dunes and you still had some lovely calm water to look out on.

As they walked along Saoirse asked, “How do you feel about moving back in with your mother and father?” “To be honest, not too bad … It is only temporary until I find somewhere else.” “Well rather you, than me”, she said. “I know, but we both know that my mother is not like your mom. Anyways, Summer is a good time to be at home, it’s busy on the farm and on any fine day after work I can run down through the field and hop into the river for a swim. I always miss that when I am living in town. Anyways Mom will have the dinner on the table every evening and the trade off is that I bring her home a bit of news. It will be grand once she doesn’t make my single status her pet project and start inviting around eligible women for the dinner as well.” Saoirse burst out laughing “I know, do you remember last years garden party where she cornered me?” “I know, that cracks me up and was one of the reasons I moved out in the first place” he acknowledged. The funny thing was, he thought to himself, was that his mother had been right on the money, but he had been too blind to see it at the time. "Ah, it was not, it was so you could have your wicked way with as many women as possible and your mother wouldn't be meeting them at breakfast" Saoirse joked. He smiled, "Could you imagine it? In her mind they would be fallen women and I would have to marry the first one to keep it all respectable. At least this time of the year she doesn't have the same time for her matchmaking, because she is busy in the garden and feeding the lads working on the farm. She will have less time for it so I should be safe enough." Giving her a nudge in the side he said, "I am sure she would love to see you up soon, she is mad about you, you know." "I will see what I can do; I suppose I could call out some evening and give her a hand with the weeding." "Anyways I keep telling myself, it's probably only for the summer as there will be plenty of accommodation available in September once the tourist season is over. Other times I am beginning to think the folk are not getting any younger and after rearing six children, it is probably about time one of us gave them a hand, or else what is it all for?"

"Now if I had my way, I would invest a bit of money and modernise the set up. But you know, I suppose the auld lad hasn't done too badly with it …" "Wow Ois, it sounds like you have actually given this some serious thought, tell me more …." "To tell you the truth Saoirse, I actually think the money might be in the expansion of Mom's garden and organics. People are so much more health conscious these days and there is a niche there that could be tapped into, especially with all the restaurants in Killarney. People are really into 'farm to fork' these days. We could even do an open farm with tours and everything if we set it up right. We are close enough to the town for that." She could hear the passion and excitement in his voice. "Careful Oisin, or the next thing you will be thinking of is taking over the farm." "Do you know, I think that's exactly what I am thinking of doing?"

Turning towards him and taking both his hands in hers. He flinched as the heat of the intimacy shot through him. It was like an electric current running up his arm.

Totally unaware she carried on saying, "My God Oisin, that's a massive step, from a steady income to taking over a farm and building it up. You will have a lot of long hours and hardship." In his head he said, "if I had you by my side I could do anything" but he just shook his hand free and said, "I don't know, I always liked the outdoors and sometimes I sit in the office listening to all that nonsensical crap and particularly on a fine day, I often think, wouldn't I be a lot better off out in the fields making my money off the land like all before me? Anyways that's the dream, for now I will be able to help Mom with the weeding in the tunnel and the garden and give the auld lad a help around the farm with the silage and everything.""You know Oisin, maybe you shouldn't dismiss it, never mind what I said about the hardship … If it's what you would really like to do, have a look into it, get a business plan together and see if it is viable. There are people who could help you with that. It's funny though; I am surprised to hear you talking of settling down. You are normally thinking up of plans to get away from the 'grind' as you call it." "You know what Saoirse I have been thinking a lot lately, that it's about time I grew up. I am 31 and will be 32 my next birthday. How many of my friends are already settled down with their own house and some with a wife and family? They all know where they are going and up to now, I really didn't have a clue. Yes, I have a good job with great pay but is it really me? When I look forward in 10 years, I just can't still see myself behind a desk. I see myself out in the garden or the fields. I see myself teaching a small boy or girl to swim and paddle the old canoe in the river like my dad taught me. I see a woman I love by my side, together sharing in everything we do. I suppose in truth my dreams are simple, I want the humble life similar to my parents. It's a good life and I have had enough of commercialism and materialism. My parents are very happy together and it was a simple but great childhood for us." He did not mention that she was the woman he envisaged by his side, but in his heart, he felt she would be.

"I don't really see the bachelor life for me." At this she raised an eyebrow and said, "up to now, you could have fooled me." "I won't deny it, I have really enjoyed my 20s but I think it's time for me to grow up and take hold of my life."

She stopped in her tracks and turned around to look at him, "Oisin, in all this time we spent together I never knew you felt like that. Are you for real or just having me on? Of all men I know, I can't believe I am hearing those words out of your mouth. Have you met someone or is there something wrong with you that you are not telling me about? That's it … your sick or something?" Reaching up she placed the palm of her hand on his forehead to check his temperature. With her standing so close it took all of his self-control not to crush her to his chest and kiss her senseless there and then. Oblivious to his personal struggles she said "No your forehead is fine, no temperature, stick out your tongue there and let me see if it's white then I will know that you are sick." He stuck out his tongue and she stood on her tip toes placing her hand on his shoulder to steady herself so she could see. She said, "no you're fine." Taking her hand and turning to face him he tipped her chin up and looking into her eyes, he said "I promise you I am not sick, but you are right there is someone, but not someone I met recently, more of an awakening to how I feel about her and again I promise you there is nothing wrong with me." She shook her head despite what he was saying she almost felt in that moment that he was about to kiss her. She pulled away and said "Oisin, she must be really something if she has changed you like this. What the hell are you doing here with me so and not spending the day with her?" He just smiled and said, "it's complicated but I am crazy about her'.

"Now that I have discussed my 10-year plan can we move on to another topic and I will explain when the time is right who she is .. Let's enjoy today and leave the weighty side of life aside. I will race you to the picnic spot, it's only 500 meters from here" and he raced away. Not one to let a challenge go Saoirse sprinted after him, having been a good 800m runner in her day she had almost caught him when he flopped down on a spot and said, "You must be slowing down. You were a bit off today."

She pulled out the picnic blanket and threw it at him, saying "don't mind my speed only make yourself useful and spread this out." Saoirse whipped off her top and continued, "I might as well catch some of these rays now that I am heated up after that run." With her head in her bag rummaging for the sunscreen she asked, "Would you mind putting it on my back? I don't want to go home looking like a lobster, it is not a good look for a Wellbeing Coach you know." Oisin hadn't realised he was holding his breath and staring at her until she pulled it out and said "Ah hah! Well what are you gawping at will you rub it on or not?" "No bother" he said but his hands were shaking. He couldn't believe that something as simple as rubbing on a bit of sunscreen would make him so nervous. It wasn't like he hadn't done it for her before. Get a grip man, or your game will be up he told himself. With a supreme effort at calmness he did not feel, he rubbed it on. It was more of a dabbing though and not his usual deep tissue massage which she noticed and said, "Are you afraid you are going to catch something off me or what? Will you rub it on properly?" She was totally unaware of his internal turmoil. Once he had done her back, she slathered it on the rest of her and said, "Are you taking off your top, will I do yours for you?" "No, I think I might wait until later to strip off." He was not sure if he could prevent himself from shaking if she touched him. He threw himself down on the blanket as far away from her as he could but she noticed and said "You are acting awful odd today, are you afraid I will bite you or what?" He was only giving himself the space to collect himself, but this he could not tell her, so he had to shimmy back in a little bit.

Once settled they both took out their rolls, crisps and drink and sat in a companionable silence just taking in the view in front of them. Saoirse eventually said, "I can't believe it, you finally have been hooked after all this time and now it's some big mystery. But do you know what though Oisin, I can truly say, a day out with you is never dull. This woman whomever she is; she's a lucky woman; her life with you won't be dull either. You know I kind of envy her, that's the type of life I would like myself as well." He was breath taken by her admission. He always knew she liked the outdoors and a fairly simple life, but they had never really talked that much about the future. "I suppose life is like the sea and with strong waves it can change course. The changes you are suggesting in your life are nearly as potent; to change from the merry bachelor to a homemaking organic farmer" she said. Leaning up on one elbow and twisting a lock of her hair around his finger he said, "don't you think you're getting a bit carried away Saoirse, even for you that's a bit poetic" he joked. He wasn't too sure he was ready yet to be described as a homemaking, organic farmer. "I don't think it's quite that dramatic; at some stage most men do grow up don't you know." She smiled and leaning towards him whispered "Are you sure you don't want to spill the beans and tell me who she is? Even just give me a tiny hint?" Kissing the tip of her nose he said, "All I know is she is the woman for me but she is not ready to hear it herself and has no clue about how I feel about her. When the time is right, I will make my move and until then I will try and spend some time with her. Other than that, I am not prepared to tell you anymore." "Oh, you dark horse, I always knew you were deeper than you let on but, bloody hell I never knew how deep. Well isn't it mad that the two of us should find someone at the same time and yet here we are today. To be honest for me a day at the beach wouldn't be the same without you." He laughed and thought to himself, you have no idea really do you, but I will have to be careful if I am to bide my time and we need to have less of these intimate situations. This was killing him, to be both with her and not be with her in the way he wanted to be.

After some time, they got up and headed back along the front beach stopping every now and then to admire the scenery and the views across to Inch on the opposite peninsula. As they got closer to the main bathing beach, they took off their shoes just to walk through the water. There is nothing more refreshing than the feel of bare toes squelching through the sand with the water lapping over them. The beach was much busier than when they had arrived, and the tide was turning so they would be able to hit the waves once they got back to the car. Saoirse was looking out at the other body boarders in the water and spotting one fellow in a red rash vest, "Look is that John and Dave out there?" she asked. "It is I think," answered Oisin secretly giving thanks that he would not be on his own with her for the rest of the afternoon. He was not sure that if they remained alone, that he would be able to keep his hands off her. A few times he felt an almost involuntary urge to reach out and touch her long sleek ponytail or her beautiful, toned arm. All he wanted to do was pull her into his arms and shout his love for her on top of his voice, but he knew his timing would be way off with Donal currently in her life. Instead he said, "Do you want to stake out a spot there and I will go back to the car and get the gear?" "Are you mad she said, there is too much of it, I will go back with you and give you a hand … Sure isn't there plenty of space on the beach and we will get a spot when we get back." After putting back on their shoes, they headed back to the car, up across the rocks to collect the gear. Saoirse reckoned that swimming togs and rash vest would do nicely today as it wasn't that cold. There wouldn't be any need for the wetsuit. She might as well make the most of the day and try and get a decent colour on her legs rather than the cycling tan she was sporting at the moment. It stopped in a straight line about an inch above her knee.

Pulling the necessary bits out of the car they headed back to the beach carrying their bags on their backs and their boards under their arms. Saoirse was thinking that Oisin had gone a bit quiet and she had noticed that he seemed to be keeping a bit more space than usual between them. She thought overall he was acting a bit strange, but she decided to ignore it and get on with enjoying the day. She was really looking forward to getting into the water and feeling the power of the waves rolling in as she made her way out against them. With each rolling wave there is a sense of exhilaration, and Saoirse always reckoned there was no better abdominal workout. If you were at this on a regular basis you were guaranteed a six pack she figured.

There was something therapeutic in the wild power of the roaring waves. For Saoirse, body-boarding was mindfulness at its best, all she had to do was focus on keeping her footing and wade out against the incoming waves, and then, once she was out far enough, she could relax and watch the waves build from further out. Watching each wave building from a flat sea surface is mesmerising, an amazing feat of nature. As the waves approached she reflected on how everyone has two choices similar to love, you either go with the first wave or wait out the next one hoping for a better one to come along. Once you caught that wave there is nothing like it, lying on the board, being swept into the beach, and feeling utterly weightless in the moment.

"Who's for a sup of tea after that?" Oisin asked. Having stayed in the water for some time, they were frozen. "Count us all in, I'd say" said Dave looking around at everyone, "and if you have any of your mothers buns you would make our day." "Well your in luck lads, I think you might even get two, she was generous today." With the tea and the buns devoured, and everyone warmed up, the lads headed up the beach to have a game of soccer and warm up.

Saoirse decided to relax on her beach mat for a while. She had a good book which she was reading at the moment and decided that she would take a break from the activity and leave the lads at it. She could have joined in the game if she wanted as she had some serious soccer skills, but she decided relaxation in the sun was a luxury that they didn't often get in May. She picked up the book but couldn't really concentrate on the story, so she put it back down again to look around her.

A couple walking a dog caught her eye. The dog was a beautiful golden retriever who was diving into the water to catch a ball thrown by the man. He emerged from the water shaking droplets off himself and ran back with the ball. The woman was clearly pregnant and was glowing in a long floaty maxi dress. She was deep in conversation with the man who was smiling as he threw the ball. They seemed so comfortable and happy in each other's company. She was wondering if this was their first pregnancy or had they other children. She assumed that since they were so relaxed, contented and in harmony with one another as they walked, that it was their first.

She wondered if she would ever be part of such a couple herself. Not that she was broody for a baby but the simple contentedness of the partnership. Would Donal be that man or did her happiness lay elsewhere? Was she instead destined to be on her own? A thought struck her, of course it wouldn't be her and Donal, as he didn't even like the beach. There was no way he would be walking with her on it. Just for a moment she put Oisin in the position of the man. They were already comfortable in each other's company, loved the same things, but then she had to shake herself. Stop that, she said to herself, he is your friend, and didn't he only tell you this morning that he had found someone he was crazy about. It was funny though, while he was telling her that, she had felt a tension between them that she had never felt before and at times she actually thought he had been half-flirting with her. She gave herself a good mental shake, telling herself not to go there, she had been down that road before and nothing came of it. They were just good friends and that was all there was to it.

She lay back down to enjoy the sunshine and the beach. As she was lying there, she began to wonder who she would be doing the Ring of Beara cycle with? Would she do it with Donal or would she do it with Oisin and the lads as she always did? She supposed that she would do it with Donal, but he hadn't asked yet and she hadn't mentioned it to him. The Ring of Beara cycle was a fabulous charity cycle that started in Kenmare and went all the way around the stunning Beara peninsula. It was a lovely day out as you could do a shorter 110km cycle or a longer 140km cycle and in May she usually only felt like doing the 110km one. A few of the lads did the 140km as it was a bit more of a challenge with some serious hills and epic scenery. To the right you had the sea and to the left you had the mountains literally rising out of the road.

A ping from her phone disturbed her musing and when she checked it she saw a message from Donal, *"just home from d cycle would love 2 c u later if ur free."* Feeling mellow from the exercise and sun she was no longer annoyed with him and decided to text back *"yes if ur planning to feed me'*. He replied, *'after 2day I think I owe u that, how about 7.30 my place?" "Sure"* she responded immediately. Looking at her watch she realised it was already nearly 4pm and if she was to make a 7.30pm date she had better get a move on. Jumping up Saoirse practically skipped down the beach with a massive smile on her face. "Lads, sorry to break up your game, but I need to take Oisin as I have to get back to Killarney" she shouted. Oisin looked at her; "what's the hurry Saoirse" he asked. "You are looking at a woman who has a hot date for the night, and I need to get back to make myself beautiful." His face dropped, "I thought we were on one and you are beautiful as you are" he joked with all the humour he could muster. At that the lads gave him a bit of a ragging saying, "Oisin man, careful it's not you that has her all perked up … You will have to go man, a woman can't be kept from her date." On the way up the beach to collect their gear, Saoirse said, "Thanks for the vote of confidence but I need to get showered and changed and get the glad rags on. After all, if a man gets a rash from the beach, I don't want him getting one off me." She saw a flicker of something that looked like disappointment cross his face. Oisin said bitterly, "We better get moving so, I wouldn't like to come between a lady and true love."

Having collected their gear as she walked away, she thought she heard Dave saying "he is fucked, he has it bad and now he is playing taxi." She thought this was a strange statement but decided to leave it pass as she wasn't sure exactly who he was referring to, but it sounded very much like Oisin and herself. What did Dave know anyways, wasn't he always teasing them about being made for each other, when they were just friends.

Catching up to Oisin who was now striding up the beach towards the car she began chattering on about how much she was looking forward to spending the evening with Donal and if he might be cooking or taking her out or what they might get up to. "Oisin" she asked "are you heading into town later with the lads or what are you doing?" In his mind he said I will be crying into my pillow, but to her he said, "I might pop into town later for a pint, but I am not sure yet." Once they got into the car, he turned the radio up loud and they drove in silence. He just couldn't cope with any more Donal chat and he was afraid he would explode if she kept it up. He had heard Dave's comment as well and thought what an insensitive git. It was bad enough how foolish he felt himself, without everyone else having to rub his nose in it. Saoirse was a bit put out because they were usually never short of conversation and it was obvious Oisin was trying to tune her out. After all she had listened to all his tales of conquest, but he didn't seem to have any interest in hers or words of advice. She supposed that was just men for you, it was fine when they were doing the conquering but when the shoe was on the other foot they couldn't listen.

The radio though was annoying her; it was like a physical barrier had come up between them. He just seemed to be withdrawing further from her. Eventually she leaned over and turned down the radio and asked "are you OK? … You seem really annoyed, which is most unlike you after a day at the beach, what is wrong?" He half heartedly replied, "I'm fine, really I am, can you just drop it?" With that she knew he wasn't but to make conversation she said, "Are you still planning on doing the Ring of Beara in two weeks?" His answer was short, "Yes, I am, I'm going to do it with Dave and Sean. We are going to do the 140km." She looked at him and feeling hurt, asked "Are you serious? We usually do the 110km together. You didn't even ask if I wanted to do it?" To which he spat out "Ah grow up Saoirse, things are different this year aren't they, you are going out with a cyclist, and you will be doing it with him, won't you? Why would I even be asking you?" She felt hurt and taken aback that he hadn't even asked her and just assumed that she would be doing it with Donal. The worst of it was that, right now she had no partner for the day, and she wasn't sure that Donal would even want to do it with her. He would probably want to do the 140km. Half the fun of the day was who you rode with. He turned up the radio again and they drove in silence the rest of the way back to her house.

As she sat in the car she felt like crying, she seemed to be losing her best friend, and all over another guy. She was so confused, they had such a lovely morning, she couldn't figure out where it had all gone wrong. What had gotten into Oisin, he was never like this? Usually no matter what he was fun but also sensitive and caring. Not this cold creature that seemed to be trying to push her away. Instead of coming in for a cup of tea like he usually would, he just pulled out all her gear and dumped it inside of the door and said, "I will be off so, have a good evening." He practically ran down the drive and jumped into the car and sped out of the driveway. She just couldn't figure out what had gotten into him, he was acting so strange, totally out of character. He seemed really jumpy and moody. She assumed it must be something to do with the frustration around this true love. But as far as she was concerned, if that was what true love did to you, it wasn't worth it.

Oisin drove around the corner and pulled in to the side of the road. He thumped the steering wheel with his fist a couple of times and left a roar out. He was distraught, he knew he was being a real bastard, but he just couldn't cope. He had seen the confusion on her face. It broke his heart to push her away. He was madly in love with her but every time she mentioned Donal's name it was like turning a knife in his chest. He would have happily spent the evening with her, there would be no need for showering and changing or anything. They could have just gone into the Golden Nugget for a bite to eat on the way home and he would have given anything to make love to her salty, sandy, sun-kissed body once they were back at her place. Being around her at the moment and not being able to touch her or tell her his true feelings was driving him crazy, but at the same time he couldn't stay away from her. She was like a drug and it was absolutely killing him. He didn't know what he was going to do to get through the next few weeks, but he knew he would still have to bide his time and he couldn't continue acting like the asshole, he was this evening. He had to pull himself together. He told himself, he wasn't the first man to fall in love with a woman who was unavailable, but no one had ever told him it would be this difficult.

CHAPTER 9

The values we learn as children, often define who we are as adults

Having showered and changed into a beautiful multi-coloured maxi dress that defined her figure, Saoirse combed out her hair and gave herself a spritz of her favourite perfume. She figured that she looked as well as she was going to. She packed an overnight bag, because a girl had to be prepared and it sounded like she might be staying over in Donal's this evening. She decided to go all out and put in the beautiful negligee that she had bought earlier in the week and her silk nightgown. She hopped into her car and rolled down the windows, a real luxury for May in Ireland. This would be her first visit to Donal's house, and she reckoned you could tell a lot about a man by the house he kept. As far as she knew, it was his own house, and he was not renting or living with his parents. After entering the electric gates, she caught the first glimpse of the house as she drove up the driveway. She blew out a breath wondering to herself, dear me, what have I got myself into here. It was a beautiful stone fronted, sprawling mansion set on about an acre of manicured lawns and was surrounded by beautiful, old mature oak trees. The site was elevated above the lake with a spectacular view of the mountains behind it. Bloody hell she thought, he must be loaded, and this place must have cost a small fortune. Again, she wondered what the hell have I got myself into here, where did he get this kind of money? When she was talking to him on the cycle or over dinner, she hadn't gotten any sense of this kind of wealth. Is he a drug dealer or something she wondered? Maybe I should make a run for it while I still can. But Saoirse being no coward decided she was here now; she might as well go inside. After all it couldn't hurt to have dinner with him, could it? It wasn't as if she was going to disappear off the face of the planet or he was going to kidnap her or anything. Anyways both Margaret and Oisin knew where she was going and if she didn't turn up, they could send out the search party. She figured that she would finally have a story to tell Oisin, to rival his own dating exploits.

As she approached the door which was set in a large porch on the top of a flight of steps which reminded her more of a hotel entrance than a home. She thought to herself, well the porch, although a bit ostentatious, is a good idea as it offers some shelter from the rain on a bad day while looking for the keys. Many a day she had wished she had put one on her own cottage, as she rummaged through the bottom of her bag. Mind you if he has a house like this, there is probably also a doorman. She was still in shock from her first impressions when Donal opened the door. He looked amazing barefoot and in worn jeans that fitted him perfectly, and a simple shirt opened at the neck. He had that brilliant smile on his face as he said, "welcome to my place, you are looking fabulous." He leaned over and gave her a kiss on the lips and, stepping back, said "come inside, I have just put the food on for us." All she could do was stare at him as she was still dumbstruck. He was still the same Donal she had met the previous times, but he was very much at ease here. She still couldn't believe that in any of the previous times she had seen him she hadn't got an inclination that he was this well-off. He had just seemed like a regular guy. As far as she could recall he had mentioned that he grew up in South Kerry on a farm, nothing that could provide this kind of wealth.

She was beginning to feel a little bit inadequate, and some of her confidence was slipping away. In her head she began to question, what is a guy who obviously moves in very different circles doing messing around with someone like me, a middle class, private-sector employee? Is there some other hidden agenda here or what is he playing at she wondered? In her mind she was thinking 'Pretty Woman', but that doesn't happen in real life so what is going on here? She was glad that she had left her overnight bag in the car. Her seduction plans seemed silly and immature now. She was thinking with his kind of wealth, he must be used to sophisticated society women who were professionals in playing the game. Again, she was asking herself "who is he really?" Her instinct was saying, run Saoirse, you are in way over your head here. However, her curiosity was getting the better of her. She had never been in a home like this before and to be fair he seemed a decent enough sort of guy. She just needed to stop over-reacting and enjoy the evening.

As he led her into the hallway, she was taking in the doors leading off it, the space and the beautiful hand-carved wooden spiral staircase that was leading to the landing above, over which hung an amazing crystal chandelier that she assumed correctly was Waterford crystal. In the hallway itself there were two massive Mark Eldred paintings of the Park, his famous bluebells. How she loved them and had often thought of saving a few bob and buying them at the annual charity art exhibition at Christmas. In her own mind she was thinking at least he is supporting the locals. She was taken aback by the size of them and wondered if they were specially commissioned for this house. On entering the kitchen, she was pleasantly surprised that, although it was massive, it had been furnished with all the essentials, and was done in a tastefully warm and rustic way. It was like entering a different house, although large, it had character and a warm and cosy feel, less like the hotel-feel you had when entering the hallway. This felt like the heart of a home. It had a beautiful wood burning stove in one corner with timber artfully stacked beside it to give it an Austrian look. A large comfortable sofa sat in front of it with two rocking chairs on either side. Saoirse almost expected a Labrador or Irish Wolfhound to walk in and lie on the mat, but neither appeared. On the other side of this large room was the working kitchen with solid oak presses and the American-style fridge, which seemed to contrast with the decor in the rest of the room, but she assumed it was there for utility purposes. The island in the centre of the large kitchen served as both table and workspace. Overall, despite the size, it had a lived-in feel and seemed more like the Donal she felt that she had been getting to know.

To keep things on steady ground and trying not to show how overwhelmed she was she asked, "so how was your cycle today?" "It went grand, but not as well as if I had you for company. I really missed you, you know." She replied, "Well it couldn't be helped, this was beach weather and I couldn't pass up on the opportunity to go on a fine day like this, it was a pity you couldn't come." "I am serious about the rash thing you know; I have really sensitive skin. The salt on my skin from the water and the wind at the beach really irritates me if my clothes rub off it. I am also sensitive to certain detergents, soaps, shampoos and creams. It's not very manly I know to admit but I am. I cost my mother a small fortune in doctors bills when I was a child as they couldn't figure out what was wrong with my skin, but it is easily managed now that I know what I can and can't use." "Well I hope you won't be allergic to me, I had a good wash before I came over," Saoirse joked. To which he responded, "now that's a risk I am willing to take." Looking straight into her eyes and without her even realising it he had closed the space between them. With eyes locked he asked, "do you mind?" "I thought you would never ask," she replied. He dropped his mouth to hers and kissed her slowly and deeply with expertise drawn from plenty of practice. As the kiss deepened and became more intense, she felt her legs go weak and her balance go and if he hadn't been holding her, she would have stumbled. "Wow" he whispered, "I have been wanting to do that since the morning I saw you under the trees, you were majestic in your anger and had I attempted it then you would probably have knocked my head off" he laughed.

She was having some real trouble pulling herself back together to get some semblance of composure again. While her head was still reeling, in an effort to appear like she was smooth with all things romantic, she quipped "What smells so good? I thought you were going to feed me and not feed on me?" He laughed and pulled away. "I have my speciality steak, homemade chips, mushrooms in garlic butter and just in case you don't like them some roasted vegetables." "Wow a real feast" she agreed. Still a bit nervous she knew she was rabbiting on a bit, but she couldn't seem to stop herself. "This place you have is really amazing, I am half expecting a butler or a cook to appear at any moment" she continued. "No we are home alone, and I made this myself in case you are wondering. I love cooking when I get the time and especially if I have someone besides myself to feed." "Well with a place like this I thought you would have someone to do it for you." "No, I like to cook my own food as much as I can as I know what is going into it and sure wasn't, I making dinners at home when I was about 14 for the rest of the family. I actually find the chopping and peeling and preparation very relaxing. I am the eldest of four and my mother worked so I had to do the cooking when I came in from school once I was in secondary school. I do have a housekeeper and she does the groceries, but I do like to do the cooking myself."

She stopped and stared at him. "I am going to be blunt here, but how in the name of God, did someone who was cooking the dinner at 14, end up with a home like this?" she asked. "It doesn't seem to add up. Are you into something dodgy or how did you do it?" "Well if I was into something dodgy that would not be the smartest question would it?" he asked, as he smiled indulgently. "But no, I am not. In my early 20s I had an IT start-up that did very well, which I sold and made a nice bit of money out of, I am still in IT and doing OK with it." "A self-made millionaire so?" "I wouldn't say millionaire, but I am comfortable." "How come this house and why are you based in Kerry? I wouldn't have thought that it was the IT capital of the world?" "We have an office in Dublin, but as it's IT I can work from home and be based anywhere in the world. To me nowhere beats Kerry to live and with Faranfore airport out the road I really am not more than an hour's flight from Dublin if I have to be in the office."

"I love Kerry having grown up here and it's nice to be near the family and real friends I grew up with. My sister lives in town and the family are down just beyond Caherciveen." Also he sadly thought to himself, when you make some money you find out quickly enough that you have lots of 'friends' but no real friends. He had discovered the hard way, that the people he grew up with were the ones he could count on. To Saoirse he said, "so, after living in America for a while, I said that if I got back to Ireland, I would base myself out of Kerry. I bought the house when I was with Martha as I had envisioned us getting old here and filling up the house with children. The decor is more to her taste than mine, but the kitchen is my own choice" he said with pride. Bitterly he added, "I was the one that did what little cooking was done in that relationship and as I was bankrolling the refurbishment I wanted to have at least one room that felt like a home and not a hotel.

Again, his mind wandered to his mistakes with Martha, I was so blinded by her he thought, I didn't see that what she really was into was my pocket and the high life I afforded her. She had no interest in me or what was important to me. I don't think children featured much in her plans, but she played along nicely for a while didn't she he said in silent monologue. Before it all came to a head; she was staying more and more in our apartment in Dublin, which buying was all her idea. I should have known then that it was doomed as our lives were going in separate directions, but I was blinded and flattered that she would be interested in me, a lad from South Kerry. I will not make that mistake again he thought. Giving himself a shake, he said, Enough of that, I had better stay focused here or Saoirse will think I am crazy.

Just then Saoirse said "earth to Donal." She was beginning to feel uncomfortable. Something felt a bit off here. He had just seemed to wander off mid conversation and there was a blackness to his mood with it. Sorry he said smiling, you don't want to hear about my ex, and I certainly don't want to think or talk about her anymore." Saoirse could tell that Martha had scarred him well and truly and whatever went down with them, he had come off the worst of it and the damage from that relationship still lingered. Still trying to make sense of the present situation, she wondered to herself, am I the rebound or is there something else going on here? She was getting a better sense as to why he had picked her. She was the total opposite of Martha. She was certainly not a gold digger and she hadn't a clue about him, and she clearly was not a socialite either.

Having heard about his roots and how he had earned his wealth, she was more at home with him and her confidence had returned. She felt he was telling the truth and she felt less intimidated by the house. She felt the essence of the man was in his roots on the farm in South Kerry and while he might be some sort of IT tycoon it did not define him.

She decided to move the conversation to safer territory. "I must say full marks to your cooking skills, this is fantastic. It's really tasty." He smiled and said, "Well it's great to have dinner with a woman who actually eats her food." Saoirse felt that the dinner had been some sort of a test for her, which she assumed she had passed by that comment. They kept the conversation light for the rest of the meal, chatting about this and that, getting to know each other a little better. Having finished she got up to help him with the clear up. "Why don't you just relax there in front of the fire and I will clear up?" he suggested. She said that she didn't mind and helped him to stack the dishwasher.

As they were chatting, she said "So, why me Donal? With all of this you could have anyone and I am just your average plain girl." He turned and locked eyes with her, "On the contrary why not you? You are beautiful, intelligent, charming and fit. You don't play games, after all you invited me on the first 'thank you date' or should

I say dinner." "Will you say that again" she said. "Which bit." "The beautiful and intelligent bit." "Ah go away out of that, once was enough for a man to say all that, but it's true, you are beautiful you know. Also do you know that during that same dinner you never once really quizzed me about what I did, you accepted me for the person in-front of you and that was refreshing for me. I would even bet that if you knew I was wealthy you would have run a mile and I suspected that when you walked in the door this evening you were half thinking of running too. I saw it in your eyes." "Well aren't you perceptive she smiled, it's true I didn't have a clue, you seemed ordinary enough, so it never occurred to me to check out your bank balance. When I walked in here this evening it was intimidating because I wasn't expecting it." In her own head she was saying, well you can thank my mother for not asking. Growing up I heard so much from her about how much this one had and the other hadn't that I had made a solemn promise to myself never to measure a person by their bank balance. That's not to say, when I walked in Mom's voice was not in my head. Unaware of the voices in her head Donal continued "You know what after Martha I came to the realisation that I was not for the upwardly mobile." Right" Saoirse said. "I want a woman in my life that loves me and not the trimmings. That would like to settle down and have children and whom I would be proud to bring down to meet my parents and the rest of my family. I am still the farmers son from South Kerry. I would like a warm and happy home and not just a shallow materialist existence. I have tried that and it's not for me."

He stopped, took a breath and said, "Sorry Saoirse that was a bit deep and probably more than you were expecting with that question, but it is the truth. I don't know what's with me when I am talking to you, but I seem to be overdoing it a lot." Saoirse replied "Jesus, Donal, I know this is our third date and to be honest, I am not sure where we are going yet. You are scaring me a bit with all the talk of children and settling down." "Saoirse, I know what I said was heavy, but I am just being honest. I am more than willing to take our time and see where it goes but please don't compare yourself to anyone else. You are perfect as you are." She hadn't realised it, but while he was talking, he had closed the space between them again. She suddenly became aware that he was running his fingertips slowly and ever so gently up and down her exposed arms. It was exquisite, so intimate and gentle. He brought his mouth towards hers and said, "can I?" In answer, she folded into his arms and kissed him on the lips. He tightened his arms around her while continuing to massage in circles on her back deepening the pressure and drawing her closer to him. The kiss was deep and slow, as her body moulded to his; she could feel his erection against her stomach. He moaned deeply in his throat telling her all she needed to know.

As the embrace became more urgent, she could feel her need deepening. Her fingers undid his shirt buttons to reveal that wonderful, sculptured chest that lay beneath. His body was strong and toned from years of exercise and a childhood of manual labour. She let her fingers trace the hair on his chest as it dipped towards his belt buckle. Her fingers were shaking as she opened his belt, dropping his pants which he stepped out of to revel equally gorgeous, long muscular legs. As she slipped her fingers inside the top of his briefs, he gently steadied her hand and said, "not so fast, I want to look at you too." He gently slipped his fingers under the shoulder of the dress and let it drop to the floor, leaving her standing in the middle of the kitchen floor, in nothing but her underwear. In a breathless voice he said, "You are beautiful, do you mind if we take this somewhere more comfortable?" "Yes please," she assented, and taking her hand, together they climbed the spiral staircase to his bedroom.

It was a large room with a gigantic four poster bed in the centre, covered in a pristine white bedspread. On the wall hung photos from Killarney National Park taken by local photographers. He guided her to the bed and, looking deeply into her eyes, he said "are you sure about this, you are trembling?" "Absolutely … right at this moment I have never been more sure about anything, once you have protection." "Saoirse, you are so beautiful, and you don't even realise it. Opening the top drawer he fished out a box of condoms, with a promise of what was to come. His hands were also shaking as he ran them over her body. She closed her eyes and gave up her body to the sensations that were engulfing her. Everywhere his hands went his mouth followed. He gently removed her bra and panties, like he was unwrapping a precious gift. She had never felt so treasured but at the same time she wanted more. Where was the passion? She opened her eyes and began to kiss him deeper as her need to feel him inside of her was getting stronger. She pulled him down on top of her and wrapped her two legs around him, rolled him onto his back and shuddered. "Donal," she moaned, "I want you, long and hard and deep inside. Where is that condom?" He produced the condom which she seized and rolled it expertly down to the base of his penis in one fluid move. She mounted him taking him deep inside of her. "Oh, Donal" she cried "you are massive." He sat up locking her hips down hard on his and took her breast in his mouth and sucked. Throwing her head back she rode him enjoying the sensation and the liberation. They moved together in unison until their climaxes exploded, leaving them both shuddering in release. She felt her eyes slightly mist over. "Oh my god, you're crying …Did I hurt you?" he asked. "Not at all, on the contrary that was exquisite," she breathed. He was blown away by Saoirse. He had been with many women over the years, but he had never been with a woman so at home in her own body. She was like a

Goddess with flowing hair, pert breasts, a flat stomach and toned from head to toe. It was the most divine sex he had ever had.

Afterwards she just lay beside him in complete relaxation and an angelic smile on her face. She was truly beautiful. "Do you know that was the most amazing sex I have ever had in my life" he acknowledged. "Me too" she began, "but to tell you the truth, I was bit worried that I might not be too good at it as I haven't had a lot of practice." "Saoirse my dear, you are amazing, that was mind blowing. I feel privileged to have shared that experience with you." She turned to him and kissed him, saying "Thank you, how do you fancy a re-run?" He said "I am ready if you are" and he kissed her long and slow and deep. This time it was beautiful, gentle and languorous lovemaking. Saoirse was completely relaxed and fell asleep afterwards.

Donal was lying there thinking he couldn't believe it. He felt like he had won the lotto. Saoirse was exactly the woman he needed in his life. She was everything he was looking for. She was beautiful, intelligent, and great to be with, into the things he was and would be a great partner in life. He could see it already. The house teaming with little people and him coming home after a day in Dublin and Saoirse having the dinner ready and all the children excited to see Daddy. It was an old-fashioned dream he knew, but when you had everything else what more could you dream of? He loved his nieces and nephews and the fun and the life in his sister's house. He felt that his life was empty. He had everything money could buy but he didn't have someone to come home to and he often felt so lonely in this big, sprawling house. He also felt that Saoirse would be fabulous in the role of executive wife, helping with the little entertaining he did or when attending the odd party that was mandatory if he was to do business. Anyways he thought, I better not get too far ahead of myself as I nearly terrified her earlier this evening when I mentioned family and settling down; he had seen the fear in her eyes. He would have to take this easy if he wanted it to last and let her get to know him a little bit better, get more used to his lifestyle before he made any more references to children and a long-term plan. He rationalised to himself that at this point in his life he would be a fool to just focus on the romance, he had to be realistic, he wanted more and he was putting his cards on the table. Neither of them were getting any younger.

If he was to assess the situation with his business brain, he knew there were some risks, particularly competition from her friend Oisin, obvious from the way she talked about him. He would like to see them together and then he would be able to tell what their relationship really was about. To him it seemed to be a bit more than friends despite what she said about them being 'just friends'. Oisin seemed to be involved in every aspect of her life. His name popped into so many conversations, the garden, cycling, walks and most social occasions that she attended, even this morning they were able to just meet up immediately, after she had completely changed their plans for the day. To him Oisin seemed like a man who was more than available to Saoirse and that meant he was the competition. He knew that he shouldn't let his thoughts go down this possessive route. He had to take a hold of himself or otherwise the scars Martha left would wound him for life. He had to learn to trust again. After all, tonight Saoirse was in his bed and not Oisin's, and as far as he knew, based on her conversations, they had never even kissed.

The next morning when Saoirse woke up, she was surprised to see Donal's side of the bed empty. She wondered where he had gone and what he was up to. She decided that she would have a poke around and maybe even have a shower. She felt a bit stiff and sore and thought no wonder after the night they had. It had been wonderful. She never thought sex could be so fulfilling. She had a few previous experiences, but in comparison to last night she realised they were only just juvenile fumbles. A few times in the past she had been left wondering what all the big fuss about sex was for, she could take it or leave it. Now what they had gotten up to last night was amazing. She certainly would like a bit more of that in her life. As she went into the shower, she was humming to herself. It suddenly occurred to her that she had forgotten her overnight bag in the car as things had progressed. She had no clean clothes or wash bag with her. So much for a shower and freshen up she thought. Ooh, she thought going into the bathroom, he was good; all bases were covered! She found a basket on the wash-stand with a fabulous shampoo, conditioner and shower gel in it, with a sticky note saying "enjoy." There was a fabulous fluffy towel on a heated rail with a thick, soft robe hanging on the back of the door. Wow, she thought, he is either really used to entertaining women or he went out and got these especially for me. My standards were low before this she thought. The shower was amazing with powerful jets massaging her scalp and shoulders. Closing her eyes, she completely relaxed as the water cascaded down. It was relaxing and invigorating in equal proportions. She wasn't familiar with the brand of shower gel, but it smelt fabulous and expensive. She was thinking to herself that she could get used to this life.

Wrapping herself in the fluffy robe she wandered down the stairs to try and find Donal. As she got to the foot of the stairs, she decided to follow the sound of music that she could hear blaring somewhere. Half-way down the corridor a door was slightly ajar. This was where the music was coming from and peering around it, she found a fully stocked gym with ropes, kettle bells, medicine balls, weights, treadmill and a bike on a turbo trainer. There Donal was working on squats with a bar across his shoulder

control and began to thrust deeply; she clenched her legs around him opening completely to host his manhood. Just as she screamed out on climax he shuddered and released into her consummating their lovemaking. Wrapping his arms around her, he gently tugged her robe back in place holding and kissing her as if she was his most treasured possession.

As she came to her senses, she felt a dribble down her leg and her sense of pure elation was immediately replaced by utter panic. "Oh my God Donal, we didn't use a condom, did we? I can't believe it, I could be pregnant. Bloody hell what were we thinking?" Hysterically she cried "I told you last night there was no sex without a condom." In a calm voice he asked, "are you on the pill?" "No, I bloody well am not, I can't see the point of putting hormones into my body regularly when I am generally not getting laid. I can't believe you didn't have a condom and you obviously came down with intent in that robe. I made myself clear or at least I thought I did last night that there was no sex without a condom." "Calm down and don't blame me, you didn't stop me, I asked and you … and you said yes, so I assumed it was OK, most of the other women I have been with have looked after themselves so I assumed you were on something. I did have the condom in my pocket in case I needed it." "Jesus Christ Donal," she spat at him, "I am not like your other women, I don't sleep around, and I expected you to use the condom."

"You can't lay all the blame on me, you were as much into this as I was, so don't go all it's a man's responsibility now to take the lead. It's the 21st century you know, and you are no shrinking violet." "Shut up Donal for fuck sake," she shouted "this is a disaster, and you are making it worse, I don't want to be pregnant, not now and maybe not ever. I am not ready to be a mother and I don't want to have a child with you, I don't even know you." "Calm down" he said "we can get the morning after pill, it's not the end of the world. Surely you could see I wasn't wearing one." She burst out crying, "I can't believe I could be so stupid. I trusted you, I thought you were different, I thought you cared but you are just like every other man thinking with your dick." "Come on Saoirse, this is not the dark ages … anyway, I think we would make excellent parents," he said jokingly, "… don't you?" "That's not the point," she roared. "That is a decision you make together and not just do it and see what happens. It's Sunday, where am I going to get emergency contraception? I don't think there is any pharmacy open."

"Don't panic, you can get it tomorrow, haven't you got 5 days or something like that, now?" "Alright for you, it's not your body," she roared, "typical, it is always the woman who is left carrying the baby." "For God's sake Saoirse you are totally over reacting, it's not the 1800's, you have a choice, the morning after pill or even keeping it." Pushing him aside as she headed for the door, she said "Get out of my way, I am out of here." "Hold on, you can't go out in just a robe, I will get your bits from the car."

When he came back in, she was standing at the counter-top, with her head in her hands sobbing. He placed his hand on her shoulder and said, "I am so sorry, believe me I never meant to hurt you, I just got caught up in the moment and didn't think. For what it's worth I think I am falling in love with you." She shook his hand off, grabbed the bag and headed for the bathroom. When she came out of the bathroom, he could see she had splashed water on her face. "I am leaving now, and I don't want to see you again," she stated. "Are you sure you are OK to drive, can I at least drop you home?" No way, she thought, and leave her car here. He must be joking. "No" she said coolly. "I am leaving, and I won't be back." Driving down the driveway the tears returned, and she felt like such a fool, the worst thing was she had trusted him explicitly to have her welfare in mind. It was her own foolishness that upset her the most. How could she have been so naive? She felt that in some way he had trapped her with all his talk of family and home. She began to wonder had he actually planned it? Was he that desperate to have a child that he would have unprotected sex with anyone? Surely not, she thought to herself, but you really just wouldn't know. She began to focus on her situation, to figure out what she was going to do to resolve it. She could go to the out of hours GP service, but could you imagine the conversation. I had mad sex with an amazing hot guy, it was so good that we forgot to use protection and I might be pregnant. No way she thought, she would be mortified, that was like something a teenager would say or do. She was a grown adult and should have more cop on. She couldn't even blame it on the drink. It really was passion, but she had to admit that it had been amazing until she realised he hadn't used protection. God, he must have thought she was completely unsophisticated. What was it he said "anyone else he had been with looked after themselves." Mother of God she thought, what had she been thinking to get herself into this situation? She certainly hadn't been using her head, they talk of men thinking with their penis, but she must have been thinking with her vagina.

CHAPTER 10

Life's lessons can be hard to take, but with each one we get new perspective

She decided that she would go home, calm down and ring Margaret. It would be good to get a bit of sensible perspective on the whole situation. Really it was her own fault, but should she see him again? To be fair to him he was a very attentive lover, she had really liked him, and he had apologised. What was hurt, was her pride really, but could she face him again after over reacting like that. She couldn't ring Oisin she thought, as this was a woman's problem and he would laugh at her for being so stupid. God, she felt like a total fool. She had totally over-reacted, but it had been blind panic. Just as she got to her door her mobile pinged with a message from Oisin *"fancy a short cycle round d lake 2day."* She thought to herself, that might actually be what I need, to have a bit of craic with him and forget about my current situation.

She replied, *"sure what time will u b here? I assume we will start from my place." "B right over"* he replied. That would give her about 20 minutes she thought. She dashed off to shower and change into her cycling gear which was easy as it was a fine day. All she needed was shorts and a t-shirt and one water bottle would do, as it was a short cycle. She still felt a bit shaky in herself and she hoped Oisin wouldn't notice. As she was getting her bits together, he rang the doorbell and walked in. She came out to the hallway to say, "hi, that was good timing, I could do with a bit of fresh air." He took one look at her and said, "What happened? You don't look like a woman full of the joys of new love, in fact you... look like you have been crying." At this she burst out crying and he was immediately over to her, wrapping her in his arms and drawing her against his chest. "What the hell happened, what did he do to you?" he asked. She could hear the anger in his voice and feel the tension in his body. Unable to get words out she just bawled all the harder. "If I see him, I will fucking kill him," he said. "What did he do to you? What happened? Are you OK?" Through her sobs she said, "it was my own fault, not all his." At this stage he was barely keeping his anger in check, his mind was running away with itself, had Donal forced himself on her, or got her to do something that she didn't want to? If Donal was in-front of him, he would have punched his lights out for upsetting Saoirse like this. He had known her for years and never seen her so upset.

Taking a breath and in as calm a voice as he could muster, he said "Saoirse darling whatever has happened, please tell me and I will try to help you." As she began to pull herself together, she began to explain that it was an amazing night and morning, they had amazing sex, but there was a possibility that she was pregnant as in the end they had sex without protection. She was at pains to explain that she had made a total fool of herself and ran out the door. He could feel every word she said like a physical blow to the chest. Whatever he was expecting, he wasn't expecting this. This was his Saoirse, the woman he loved, telling him she might be carrying another man's child. He wanted to punch something, best of all if it could be Donal. It was painful to hear but he had to help her out here. It could have been worse, at least he hadn't raped her or something. He said, "That's not so bad Saoirse, I thought he had hurt you, there is a simple answer to that problem, go to the doctor tomorrow and get the morning after pill." He couldn't believe she was making such a fuss over something that was easily fixed. "Not to be crude here" he said "but if ye went hurling without a helmet, you might have more problems than pregnancy. Chances are if he has done it once he has done it many times." "Oh my god" she said, "I was so focused on pregnancy that I never thought of getting a disease … Oh Jesus Oisin, how was I so stupid, what am I going to do?" In a completely matter of fact reply he said "Take a half day tomorrow and go to the doctor, is what you are going to do." "Oh my God, I will be totally mortified, but you are right." "If you want, I can take a half day off and go with you if you like?." She looked at him and said, "Would you really do that for me even though you had no hand, act or part in this situation, you know they would think it was you?" Without a blink he said, "What are friends for? Well I don't mean actually go into the doctor with you but I could drive you and go for coffee afterwards if that would help?" In his mind he was thinking well at least I would know you did something about it. Feeling much better she smiled and said, "Well you really are my best friend and it's good to know I can count on someone, are you on for that cycle, I certainly could do with some head space..

She went back into the kitchen to get her keys off the worktop and as she did, she had a mental picture of herself and a little girl of about five at the counter-top making iced buns. She had to pinch herself. She had never really thought about her future before. She was happy going to work, spending time with friends, cycling, gardening and going on the odd date. She had never really pondered what she would be doing in ten years or even five years' time. She was just happy in the here and now. For a brief moment she thought maybe I should take my chances and see what happens. It would be lovely to have a little toddler wrapping its chubby arms around my neck and say "Mama I love you." If I get the morning after pill will I always be wondering what might have been.

Just as she was giving herself a mental shake, Oisin said "are you sure you are up to this. You seem very far away." "To tell the truth" she said "I was just thinking will I take my chances. Having a child wouldn't actually be the worst thing in the world at my age. It might be the only chance that I get." "Ah Saoirse" he said, "you can't be serious, have you lost your mind?" "Well obviously I would get the STI test, but I think I might skip the morning after pill. Anyways it's at least nearly three weeks since my last period so I should be fine. I don't think there is any need to be putting unnecessary hormones into my body." "Well for what it's worth I think you are absolutely crazy, but it's your decision," he replied.

"Now are we going for this cycle or not?" "I must get my phone and I will be right out" she said. She had a look at her phone, and she had a message from Margaret *"any chance you would mind the lads for me this evening, I am really stuck, and I need to go to a funeral."* Saoirse replied, *"sure, what time do you want me over at"; "in the next hour or so if that is all right."* She came out of the kitchen holding the phone up saying, "Oisin I am really sorry to do this to you, but I have to pull out of the cycle Margaret is stuck for a babysitter and she wants me over there in the next hour." "Do you want me to go with you?" "Ah no Oisin, why don't you go on and enjoy the cycle. If you want, you can call back here afterwards, I will probably only be over there for a few hours. "I might do that," he replied. "I will leave the car here so if that is alright with you." Saoirse was humming away to herself as she changed yet again into a comfortable top and leggings to go over to mind the children. She loved minding Margaret's kids, Sarah was 5 and Niall was 7 and they were two real cuties. They loved when she came over and played chase with them or pushed them on the swing. Saoirse was able to give them her full attention, unlike their mother who had a million and one jobs to do, just to keep the house running. She didn't know how Margaret did it, she kept a full-time job going, ferried the children around to activities and managed to keep a fairly clean and tidy house. She somehow managed to fit in yoga and a gym class during the week. She really was super woman in Saoirse's eyes. She wondered would she be able to do all that too, if she was to have a child. Saoirse usually brought over a little treat for the kids. They really appreciated it as Margaret was very strict on the treats. She only bought them on Saturday when they went to town and they didn't get them any other day. She was of the opinion that once a week was more than enough. Saoirse always liked to sneak them something, although she was sure Margaret was well aware, as nothing got past her. She rationalised that chocolate wasn't too bad as at least there was milk in it, and it didn't drive them crazy like the jellies.

She wondered if she should tell Margaret about her morning. She decided not to as really when she thought about it, what was there to tell! Other than that, she had really great but unprotected sex, and now she might be pregnant or have an STI. She decided to keep that bit of information to herself and she would go to the doctor tomorrow and just get on with it. The whole country didn't need to know her business. It was bad enough already, that Oisin knew, but at least he was willing to help her. She began to think about him for a minute. There was something slightly off or different about him lately. Soirse couldn't quite put her finger on it. Maybe it was this unrequited love, but, in some way she felt he was acting different with her. Even earlier when she was upset, he seemed to be really angry, she had felt him vibrating with it as he comforted her and his offer to go to the doctor with her seemed a bit much. She could talk to him later she supposed and try and see what was going on with him.

Just as she was leaving, she heard her phone ringing and she was wondering who it might be. Looking at the screen she saw it was Donal and decided to let it ring out. Once the phone stopped ringing a message pinged through indicating that he had left a voicemail. She pressed play on the message and heard him say "Saoirse, I am so sorry, I never meant to hurt you, I just got carried away this morning, I am really worried about you, did you make it home OK, can I call over?" Without thinking she texted back '*I am fine, no hard feelings, no need to call over*'.

When he saw the message, he was really disappointed. He had expected more from her, this avoidance seemed childish and that was a blow-off if he ever had one. This whole situation was a disaster and it had had such potential. He had really liked her; they had got on so well. They had a lot in common and, to add to that, they were a perfect fit in bed. He was raging at himself. He couldn't believe how careless he had been. He simply hadn't thought, he had been totally carried away in the moment this morning. Making love with her was elemental; she was so free and unrestrained. When she had lost it afterwards, he was totally taken aback and couldn't think straight. He had said all the wrong things and just made the situation worse. He had even foolishly mentioned that other women looked after themselves. He was lucky she hadn't taken his head off after that. He had never been in this situation before, he was always so careful with protection. His father had taught him to respect himself and the women he was with. He was so disappointed in himself. He had never had sex before without protection as there was more than pregnancy to be worried about. With Saoirse it was different, all rational thought was lost. He had seen her standing there at the door in the light and his intention had only been to wrap his arms around her, and breathe her in. She had looked majestic. He had been totally captivated by her. After all his talk about a wife and family she was bound to think that he had planned it, and nothing could be further from the truth. It was only three dates and he had to admit that he was totally madly head over heels in love with her. Now she wouldn't even answer his calls.

He decided to go into the gym and work off his frustration, it was the only way he knew that he would be able to sleep tonight. He would have to wear himself out. He tore into the ropes and punished himself. He pumped iron for all he was worth but still didn't feel the escape. He then turned to the treadmill where he knew he would keep going until he collapsed. Practically crawling from the gym, he threw himself down on the couch and mindlessly watched television. At some point he dozed off, because when he woke, he was frozen stiff and aching from dried up cold sweat and overworked muscles. He couldn't be bothered with proper food and just got a bowl of cereal and went to bed. He could still smell her on his sheets and her discarded dress was lying on his floor. He knew it was going to be a bad night but what could he do now? He had tried to call her, and she wouldn't take his calls. He would have to give it a day or two for her to cool off and then try again.

CHAPTER 11

Asking for help when we need it is a sign of strength not weakness

Oisin headed off for the cycle but he couldn't get Saoirse's tear-stained face out of his mind. He would really kill Donal if he met him. He loved her so much. It was difficult to hold her in his arms and not kiss her, but their relationship was not there yet. When he saw her crying, he had been terrified something really bad had happened to her. In all their years of friendship he hadn't really seen that vulnerable side of her before. His need to protect her had been instant. Once he heard the story though, he had felt that she was making a big song and dance of the situation, but he assumed it was the subconscious conditioning from her upbringing that had her in such a flap. He really hoped she would go to the doctor in the morning and sort things out. He didn't fancy rearing another man's child; it was not in the plan but then again, the plan was only recent, and it could always change. It would be a small price to pay to be with the love of his life. Pity I hadn't figured that out sooner and then none of this mess would have happened, he thought to himself. This situation is a way more difficult and complex than I thought it would be, he acknowledged to himself. He had initially thought all he had to do was bide his time and her relationship with Donal would run its course like most flings. He hadn't bargained on dramas or the complications of an unplanned pregnancy. He desperately wanted to tell her how much he loved her, but the timing was off. He still hadn't figured out how he was going to do it. He acknowledged that this cycle was pointless without her and really it was the last thing he felt like doing right now. He didn't have the energy for it and his heart certainly was not in it. He had only suggested it to spend some time with Saoirse.

He decided to call his brother and see if he would go for a few pints, he knew that Padraig's wife and girls were gone to some dancing competition this weekend. The girls were excellent dancers and were often away at weekends. Padraig agreed to meet him for a few. Heading into the pub, Padraig said, "Oisin if you don't mind me saying your attire is a bit strange for an afternoon drinking. What's the story?" "Yeah I know, I was out on the bike and it wasn't doing it for me so I thought maybe a few pints might hit the spot." Not a man to beat around the bush Padraig said, "Well spit it out so, what's eating you? You didn't call me in here for nothing and then turn up in that get up, so it must be bad whatever it is." "Ah, Padraig couldn't you let me warm up to it at least. I was hoping to be at least halfway down a pint before the interrogation started." "Well if you get it off your chest it will lighten your load and then we can have a bit of craic, but right now you look like the mother of sorrows." Oisin took a deep breath and said, "It's Saoirse and I don't know what to do." "Jesus, Oisin, you haven't gone and got her pregnant, have you? … I didn't think the two of ye were in the sack together." "No, we are not and that's the problem" Oisin said. "I have just realised she is the woman for me and now she is seeing someone else and, to make matters worse, she might be pregnant by him and doesn't want to do anything about it." Padraig burst out laughing and gave him a thump on the shoulder and said, "Ah Ois, you did make some cock up of this one didn't you, talk about not knowing you have a good thing until it's gone. The two of you have been crazy about each other for years. I know you always said that you were just good friends, but a blind man could feel the chemistry between the two of ye, never mind anyone with a pair of eyes. What's the story with her and this other fellow? How serious is that?" He laughed and continued, "You are some tosser you know Oisin, all this crap you spouted over the years about this being the 21st century and couldn't a fellow and a girl be friends and so on, and now look at you? You really made some balls of this one man."

"Padraig. I know you think it's hilarious but this is no joke, I am heartbroken, struggling to eat and sleep here and I feel like it's all falling apart." "Ah don't be dramatic, get a bit of perspective Oisin man, how long are they at it? I don't think it's a lost cause yet, why did she come to you with her sob story?" Padriag asked. "She didn't come to me, I called out to her place and I could see she was upset. When I asked that is what she came out with. I was completely floored, and do you know what, I don't think she is going to do anything about it. Do you know what she said that this might be her only chance to have a child? Isn't that the maddest thing you ever heard?" "Based on that so she mustn't be holding out much hope for things going too far with your man so is she" Padraig replied. "Well they slept with each other last night and reading between the lines I'd say he knew what he was doing. Saoirse seemed fairly into him, but I am not sure about him. He went off cycling yesterday instead of going to the beach with her. I mean what kind of an amadán would pass up on the opportunity to see her in a bikini and rub sunscreen into that fabulous body?"

"Stop there Oisin, spare me the details, I don't need to hear your own fantasies and I am sure you obliged anyways. Tell me, do you think this is just a fling or is there more to it than that?" "To tell you the truth Padraig, I don't know, all I know is that it's tearing me apart." "In all seriousness," Padraig began, "if you want my advice Oisin bro, if I was you, I would grow a pair of balls and go and tell her how you feel. She is not a mind reader and is too good of a woman to let slip between your fingers without a fight … If I was you, instead of drowning your sorrows here with me, I would go back to her place and tell her how you feel, then the ball would be in her court. After all, for how many years have you been saying ye are just friends and you know what, now to come to think of it, I don't think I ever heard her say that? You might be surprised to learn she might feel the same way you do." "Christ Padraig, I can't just barge in there now and tell her, the timing is not right." "Never mind timing, that's just a cop out, do you want to lose her?" "I do not." "Well then if I was you, I would get your sorry lycra ass up off that stool and go home and tell her." "Well I can't right now as she's over minding Margaret's children and in the current situation, I think the timing is off." "Like I said, never mind the timing, this is not the movies you won't be having any music or drum-rolls in the background. This is real life and you just have to man up to it and swallow your pride. To my mind you're a chicken when it comes to anything meaningful, for all your experience with women. What are you actually afraid of? That she says 'no'? That's the worst that could happen isn't it?" "No" replied Oisin "that I could lose my best friend as well." "You would want to be careful based on what you said earlier, I think Saoirse's biological clock is starting to tick. That's a dangerous thing Oisin, you know when that happens, I am telling you. When a woman gets to a certain age, she wants a child and they tend to settle for whoever is in front of them. They get less fussy if you know what I mean. I think it's the sperm they are after rather than the romance. That's not to say that they stay with the guy forever, but they can settle down for a while. If you hang around too long you might have to wait a lot longer. Believe me, life is too short to be sitting on the fence on something that matters this much. Now that's all I am going to say on that, it's up to you now," Padraig finished decisively taking a sup from his pint.

"Well I came for advice and you certainly gave it … By the way, how are your girls anyways?" "They are all fine. They are gone off dancing and I had a bit of peace for myself." Prior to Osisn's call he had planned on doing a bit of gardening and then heading out home for dinner, to see the folks. "I heard you are thinking of giving up the job and joining the home crew," Padraig stated, changing the subject. At this Oisin brightened up. "I have been giving it a bit of thought lately alright. I think it could be a viable business with a bit of a change and some effort going into it. I think organics is the way to go. Sustainable food production and all that. I really don't see myself in an office in 5 years' time let alone 10, so if I am going to make a move, I need to do it now." "Have you spoken to the folks about this?" "Stop asking dumb questions," Oisin said "you know I have, how else did you get wind of it?" "Ah you know our place, once one of us has a story everyone else has it as well. Which, by the way, Mom is really worried about you. She said that you are going around the place with a face as long as a wet week and that you are taking the head off everyone. She said that you haven't been on a night out in the best part of a month and that when she asked you to bring Saoirse to dinner the other day you nearly ate the head off her." "Padraig, I do know what they are like and I also know that you can be a good man to keep things to yourself so can I please count on you to keep this to yourself. I really don't want them all dissecting my business or telling me what to do on this." "You have my silence for a week, fortnight tops" replied Padriag "and by then you better have done something about it. Even if she says no, at least tell her how you feel, otherwise how is she supposed to know how you feel about her. Also remember what I said about women and the biological clock, I wasn't joking there. Now I am away off out to Mom's for a bit of grub, do you want to come too?" "No, you're alright, I couldn't face the interrogation at the moment; I think I will stay here and have another one or two." "Well make sure it's only one or two, don't get too pissed, you know you can't handle it and you might end up doing something you regret." "Alright boss" Oisin replied, "and see you around. Thanks for the pep talk and not a word to any of the rest of them."

Oisin had a couple of more pints. While he loved a good night out, he wasn't much of a drinker, so after about seven or so he was fairly well on. With the courage of alcohol, and Padraig's words ringing in his ears, he concluded it was now or never. He was going to talk to Saoirse and tell her how he felt for once and for all. Without giving it any more thought, he called a taxi as he was in no fit state to drive over to Saoirse's. Thankfully he didn't have long to wait or he could have lost his nerve. When he got to the door, he straightened himself up to his full height and buzzed the door. After all he had a job to do and he was no coward as Padraig had suggested. Waiting at the door he gave himself a pep talk, "it's no bother man, you got this, just tell her the truth, what's the harm that can come of it." He could do this. Saoirse opened it and took one look at him and said, "what the hell is wrong with you?" "Are you pissed, you were supposed to be going for a cycle?" This was a first she thought, he has never arrived on my door before after a feed of drink, but she supposed his car was outside. "Got something to tell you" he slurred. As she led him to the sitting room, she said "I thought you were going for a cycle, how are you in this state?" Of his response all she got was "Boring without you, called Padraig," and he burped. That was even stranger she thought, as himself and Padraig were not actually that close, and they certainly were not drinking buddies. Also, she hadn't known Oisin to go to a pub on a Sunday, he was usually doing something active, or helping out at home. This carry on was way out of character. She was seriously beginning to worry about him. He was acting so strange lately. She couldn't imagine Padraig drinking himself to oblivion on a Sunday afternoon either. Whenever Padraig came up in conversation in the past Oisin always said that Padraig was the sensible, boring older brother, but come to think of it, he also said that he was a good man to have in your corner if you were stuck. Christ, she thought, things must be really bad, maybe her instinct that something was wrong on the beach was right, maybe he was sick or something and this story about unrequited love was all made up as a decoy. Anyway, it would have to wait until tomorrow. "Something to tell you," he slurred. Ignoring him she steered him towards the couch and said, "Lie down there on the couch, before you fall down. I will make a cup of tea." "Saoirse," he slurred " … need to talk." "Well" she replied, "it's obvious that you need to talk to someone, but I think it had better wait until tomorrow." He straightened up and with deep concentration got the words out, "I love you, you are the one." "Ah for God sake Oisin" she said, "you're drunk and you don't know what you are saying … Lie down there and I will get you a cup of tea." When she got back into the sitting room, he had fallen asleep on the couch. She threw a blanket over him and headed off to bed herself.

She couldn't sleep. Her mind was spinning after having such a crazy day. What with the morning panic, two men declaring their love, one talking about her potential to be a wife no less and they hardly knew each other? However, it was Oisin's declaration of love that was really playing on her mind. How many times had they talked about their friendship being only that 'a friendship', and why was it that a man and woman couldn't be friends without everyone else assuming there was more going on in the relationship. Wasn't it only yesterday that he had been telling her about this mystery woman who was the love of his life? With the drink he must have been imagining she was someone else. But then she thought what if he was really serious, hadn't he slurred something that sounded like, "need to talk" a few times before his final declaration of love, which she had ignored because of the state of him? How did she feel about that? She had to admit that it intrigued her and scared her a little, clearly, they were compatible, but was there chemistry, was he a friend or deep down did she love him too? Would they be still friends after this? She had certainly fancied him when she met him at first, but he had steered their relationship down the path of friendship, and she had happily gone along with it. At the time she had been looking for someone to do things with and the romance of it all didn't really bother her too much. Yes she would have definitely taken it, she admitted, if it had been on offer at the start but they had given each other such happiness through friendship, that she felt she didn't need any more from him now. In many ways they had been there for each other more than many couples would be for one another. She reasoned to herself that it was probably just the drink talking anyways and there was no point reading too much into it.

In addition to Oisin, Donal was also playing on her mind. What was she going to do about him? Would she see him again? Did she want to see him again? He was a really nice guy and they did get on well enough, the sex was amazing, but would she really be comfortable within his lifestyle? Could she be the wife he was looking for? What about her own hopes and dreams? Now on that point, what were her own hopes and dreams anyways? In recent times, she hadn't really given much thought to her own goals in life. Where did she want to see herself? Her choice whether to get the morning after pill or not to, was also bothering her. The more she thought about it, the more she realised that she would like to be a mother. She wasn't getting any younger, but she wondered if this was the right way to go about it. Could she do it as a single parent? She knew lots of women who were, and did a great job, but could she, Saoirse, do it? On the other hand, was her future with Donal, for them to be together as a couple? A child certainly wouldn't want for anything materially, but if the parents didn't love each other would it be a happy home? She also wondered was this a gift in disguise, could she take this mistake and turn it into an opportunity, would she get another chance to be a Mom? So many questions and only she could answer them.

She was aware that with her irregular period she most likely was not going to get pregnant that easy anyways. Her mother and father would go bananas initially, but they would get over it and support her. She could just imagine her mother with a little child on her lap, rocking it and telling stories of life in bygone days or reading from little children's books. She could see her father pushing the child on the swings similar to the one he made for them as children. They would be fabulous and present grandparents once they got over the initial shock, well her dad would, but her mother, who was she kidding? She knew in reality it could go either way with her mother.

She assumed that Oisin would help her out as well, hadn't he helped her out with everything else for the last few years, and sure there was Margaret as well. She probably should have told her today but with the kids in and out there really was no time and Margaret had seemed a bit stressed, so she had left without telling her. She could always ring her and meet her for lunch. The conversation went round and round, and on and on in her head, she couldn't get to sleep, and she tossed and turned all night.

Eventually she nodded off, but in the morning, she woke feeling utterly physically and emotionally exhausted. She could not face work and anyways she had to go to the doctors. She called her boss to let her know that she would be taking the day off. She knew that there was no way she could face work today. After the doctors, which she was dreading, she would need a good sleep to straighten herself out. She would be mortified, but she would have to face the music and do it. She decided that she had better go and check on Oisin to see if he was alright. To her surprise, when she opened the sitting room door, other than the smell of stale drink and the folded blanket, there was no trace of him. Wow, she thought, that is strange and most unlike him to have left without saying goodbye. She looked out the door to see if his car was there but that was gone too. She rang him, but he didn't answer.

When she got home later, she texted him '*been 2 d doctor, scarlet, where did u disappear 2? R u alright?*' To which he replied immediately, *'Fine, but shouldn't u b telling this 2 Donal'.* What the hell was wrong with him she wondered, there was an edge of nasty in there that was unusual for Oisin? Yesterday hadn't he been like, sure I'll go with you. She began to think about him. He seemed to be under some sort of strain lately. He was acting very strange and irrational lately, but the maddest of all, was his drunken declaration of love. She did think he had a point though, she should probably be reporting her doctor's visit to Donal, especially the decisions she had made there as it involved him, but she was too embarrassed to face him. She had made a complete fool of herself in his place Sunday morning. In fairness, in hindsight, she had totally overreacted, but it had been blind panic. She assumed having given him the blow off, he would leave her alone and she wouldn't see him anymore.

Throughout the day, Saoirse had been playing on Donal's mind. He wondered what she had done? Had she gone to the doctor. Surely, she had, he still couldn't believe that she had not been on the pill or her insane reaction to the 'situation'. He acknowledged to himself that he wasn't yet prepared to give up on her. He knew she was highly strung but despite that he felt there could be something good between them. He knew it was pointless texting or ringing her as she was stubborn and would not pick up the phone while she was still annoyed with him. He could try a blocked number, but he reckoned she wouldn't answer that either. His best bet was probably the direct approach, to call over to her house. That was a problem though, as he had not been invited and she had as of yet not even told him where she lived. He knew finding her address could be easily done. He worked in IT after all but it didn't take a genius to work out that a trawl of social media should give him the answer. He also knew it wouldn't exactly be right and proper to just show up ... and she would probably go mad. It would be a risky approach, but he decided he had nothing to lose at this stage and everything to gain.

Pulling out his phone he had a flick through her Instagram and Facebook feed. As he searched, he realised she was careful. She had lots of pictures of herself at various events and of course loads of active photos, but very few of her in her home. It annoyed him that so many of her pictures included Oisin, or the person he assumed was Osin. It was a lad she seemed to be pretty intimate with. You could tell by the body language in the pictures that they were close. Looking at these photos he could see Oisin was going to be serious competition no matter what she said about them being just friends. 'Bingo,' he said to himself, 'I know how to get it'. Of course, she was into cycling, her Strava, if she used it, it would give her address away. Why hadn't I thought of that initially he wondered. It didn't seem like she was currently posting anything with it, but he decided to go back a bit to when it first became fashionable. He knew most cyclists used it at some stage. 'There it is!' he said to himself when he found it. Three posts she had shared from Oisin's page about two years ago. Looking at the routes he could see they all started and finished in the same place. He knew from conversations he had with her that it was roughly in the vicinity of where she lived. With a knowledge of online privacy issues, it always amazed him how many people didn't protect their privacy online. Well, I have her address now, so all I have to do is call over. Maybe I will give her another day or two to cool off, but I will send some flowers. He knew it was clichéd but wasn't it an age old way of seeking forgiveness and he needed that.

CHAPTER 12

One of life's small pleasures, is to give and to get

Tuesday evening, just as she was about to leave work, Saoirse got a call from reception to say that there was a delivery for her. She was a bit annoyed as that meant she would have to traipse all the way over there and collect whatever it was and bring it back, delaying her exit. She supposed she had better get it anyways, since she took the call. When she got to reception, she saw a beautiful bunch of flowers sitting on the receptionist desk and she assumed they belonged to Megan, the receptionist. "Have you a parcel for me?" she asked. Megan smiled and said, "I sure do, would you like to take these beauties home with you? They have your name on them and the smell is divine, I was actually hoping you might have gone home and I might get another day out of them." Saoirse took a better look at the bouquet; it was a beautiful bunch of soft cream roses with the tiniest forget- me -nots sprayed through it. They were elegantly simple and there was a note that said simply *'I am sorry'*, with a scribbled initial that looked like it could be an O or a D. The office was all a buzz with her delivery. Everyone wanted to know who they were from and if she had a special someone in her life. She said that she wasn't sure, but she assumed they were from Donal.

Although simple, they were expensive and he had the money anyways, who else would be sending her flowers to work? Come to think of it though, she wasn't sure that she had actually told him, exactly where she worked; only what she did. She assumed that he had figured it out. Forget-me-nots were one of her favourite flowers; she especially loved to see them growing wild. She had even dug them up down by the river near Oisin's mother's place and planted them into her garden a few years ago. She brought the flowers home and placed them up on her table assuming that they might be the last ones that she got. She was just rustling up some dinner, when the doorbell rang. She opened the door to be met by a flower delivery man with a massive bunch of red roses that also said, "I am sorry, can I please see you again. Donal." Wow, she thought he is eager; two bunches of flowers in one day. It's amazing how different they are though she thought, she much preferred the simpler bunch she had received in work. She thought that it was uncanny that he would have put forget-me-nots in them. How did he know that she really liked them? Anyway, she decided that she would let him stew for another day although the flowers were a nice touch.

She began to think about the Ring of Beara cycle and what she was going to do. It was only 2 weeks away and now she had no one to go with. Oisin was acting really odd and she wasn't going to do it with Donal, so what was she going to do? She assumed that she would have to do it alone and that would be so boring. She knew one or two of the girls at work were doing it, but she really didn't want to tag along with them either. They had their own group of friends and although they would welcome her, it wouldn't be the same. For the last few years, she and Oisin had done all these events together. He was great, he would come over a few days before and they would have dinner together and then he would sort out her bike. Pump the tires, oil the chain and make sure everything was in good working order. He would usually come over the evening before and load up the bikes. They would go through their kit and make sure everything was there, the spare t-shirt, jellies, drinks and so forth. He would joke that they were like an old, married couple and they would have a laugh together. He would take home all her gear the night before and then all she would have to do in the morning was drive over to his place after breakfast and off they would go. God, she would miss the routine of it. She loved the build up to the event the week before, the getting ready and the banter with everyone she met who was doing it. On the day of the event itself the adrenaline buzz was unreal. She knew she could go with the girls, but it just would not be the same without Oisin.

She decided that she would meet Margaret the next day for lunch, if she was free and get some perspective on what was happening in her life. Margaret would cut straight through all the confusion, ask the difficult questions, that she was afraid to ask herself, but it would give her a sense of perspective she needed.

Saoirse decided that this evening would be a good evening to do some hill cycling. She would do the Gneevguilla loop. Spa hill would be a good test of her stamina followed by the steep climb towards Gneevguilla. From Killarney it was a good 40km loop and a nice test for the evening. She decided that she would do it on her own and take the time for herself. It was a boring enough route, but a lot of cyclists did it as you got good distance and some hills. On the climb up past Spa, a car caught up to her, she hated this as it always made her feel a bit nervous. It was a narrow, steep climb and difficult for the cars to pass. She was always afraid she would get clipped by a passing car. She pushed on up the hill and turned right for Tiernaboul and just kept pedalling the long slow, boring uphill grind. She knew that she just had to keep climbing and she would be rewarded with a downhill shortly. She had done it enough times to know this. It was one thing to do a cycle with someone else; it was another thing to do it on her own. Saoirse knew her head could really get in her way when she was on own if she left it, particularly when she wasn't feeling great. She just had to clear her head and push on.

She would take a break when she got around to Paddy O' Keeffe's General Store. She loved going in there, it was like Aladdin's cave. There weren't too many places like this left in the country anymore. You could get anything inside there from children's toys, to tools, to groceries. As shopping experiences went, it was truly unique. When she was on this cycle route, she often stopped in here for a bar of chocolate or to replenish her water bottle. From here she headed back for town down by Mastergeeha soccer field and back down Spa hill again. On returning home, as Saoirse was pulling her phone out of the back pocket of her cycling top, she realised that there was an incoming call from an unknown number. She checked the phone and realised there were also two other calls from the same number that she had missed while she was out on her bike. She decided she had better take the call from whoever it was, as clearly, they were looking for her and it wasn't some hoax call.

To her surprise when she answered the call it was Padraig, Oisin's older brother. Now that's a strange one she thought to herself, I wonder what he is calling me for. "Saoirse, do you mind if I have a word with you?"

he asked. "No bother Padraig, is everything alright?" she said. "I am really sorry to be bothering you but I am fierce worried about Oisin." "Go on" she said as her heart began to hammer in her chest, "is he sick or something? I had noticed that he has been a bit odd alright lately." "Well to be honest, I think he will have to tell you the full story himself but we would really appreciate if you could call out at home to see him." "Now you are scaring me Padraig what's going on?" "Well since Monday he hasn't gone to work and he has taken to the bed. Mom has been really worried about him for a while. She said it feels like he needs to get something off his chest. She has tried having a conversation with him, but he just closes her down and she doesn't know what to do with him. She is mad with worry, it's so unlike him but he is in a bad way." "OK Padraig", Saoirse agreed "that's bad alright, but I don't understand how me calling out is going to help, he is hardly talking to me either." "Well he does need to get something off his chest and it's you he definitely needs to talk to." "Me!" Saoirse was astonished. "He took off from my place Monday without even saying goodbye after turning up pissed Sunday." "Look Sunday evening he called me to have a drink with him," Padraig replied. "I know, but I hadn't put you down for a getting pissed on Sunday type. I would have thought you would have better things to be doing, what with the girls and everything." "You're right, but never mind the pissed part right now, I knew something was bothering him, so I met him." "And do you mind me asking, are you any the wiser? What the hell is going on with him? Is he sick or something, if you know what is going on with him I would like to know what I would be getting myself into before going out to the house to see him." "All right so, maybe I should tell you but this should really be coming from him. I know I am speaking out of turn here but he told me Sunday since you started seeing your man he has realised that he is totally madly in love with you and I think he is absolutely terrified to death by it. He is scared that he will lose you to your man and it's eating him up inside." "Sweet Jesus, Padraig, is that it? Is that what is wrong with him? I'm the mystery woman? We have been friends for years and I thought we could tell each other anything, could he not have just told me himself." "I think he is only after realising it to be honest and I know he should be the one to tell you this. I hadn't meant to tell you when I got on the phone to you, I only wanted to get you out to the house to see him, so he could tell you himself, but there it is anyways, now you know. He doesn't seem to be able to get it out and I'm afraid for him."

Saoirse was totally floored; she realised her hands were sore from gripping the phone so tight and her heart was pounding in her chest. She didn't know how to take it in. She said, "Padraig, thanks for telling me, I am totally stunned, I really didn't have any idea, he mentioned it Sunday but

I thought he was so drunk that he had confused me with someone else. Oh my God I hadn't realised he felt this way. I am totally shocked; he has always gone on so much about us being friends that I had never questioned it." "I know, and I think that may be part of the problem. It's very hard for him to back down from that position. He is very proud and I think maybe he feels foolish about all the friendship nonsense he has gone on with over the years. All I can say is, he is terrified that he will lose you. Look I know this is all a bit teenage, having your big brother tell the girl that his little brother fancies her, but I'm not sorry, I feel he needs a help out here." "Well," Saoirse began, "he did try Sunday but he was pissed, so I just laughed it off and put it down to drunkenness. Maybe he wasn't that drunk after all, he clearly took it as a rebuff because Monday morning he was gone before I got up and he hasn't been answering my calls since." "Look Saoirse, all I am asking really, is will you please call out to the house and have a chat with him before he cracks up? I know the two of you have been the best of friends for years, so even if you don't feel as he does, I hope ye can see a way through this." "To be honest Padraig, I am totally taken aback by this, but I also couldn't imagine my life without him in it." "Saoirse I am really sorry to throw this at you, but someone had to do something. I hate to see him suffering the way he is and for what it's worth I think the two of ye are made for each other. Will you at least call out and have a chat with him?" and with that, he hung up.

When Saoirse got off the phone, she thought Dear God, what was she going to do about this one? Oisin, her best friend, in love with her and his brother having to tell her? She went into the kitchen to switch on the kettle, she needed a cup of tea to steady her nerves. She was shaking.

What were they like, she thought. She supposed the signs had been there all along. He had never really wanted to hear her stories about Donal, lately she had noticed that he seemed to be touching her a lot more than he used to. It wasn't much, just a hand on the back to guide her, a light tug of her hair in jest, his hand around her shoulder, and sometimes taking her hand when he didn't really need to. A few times she had also caught him gazing at her with a strange look in his eye, and, most of all, throughout the years he had been always available to her whenever she called him except this past week. Putting the bits and pieces together it was becoming a lot clearer. To be fair, hadn't he actually told her himself. Suddenly she knew who had sent her that bunch of flowers with the forget-me-knot in them. Of course, it was Oisin and not Donal. She should have known straight away. She walked over to the bunch of flowers and plucked a sprig of forget-me-knot out and stuck it in her hair. She picked up the phone and texted him. *'Oisin haven't seen much of u this week, Ill b out 2 d house in 10 mins, and we need to talk..* That would give her no time to back out. She would just go out to visit him and get to the bottom of this.

CHAPTER 13

A mother's intuition is often finely tuned to their children's needs.

His mother answered the door and gave her a big hug saying, "am I glad to see you." He is down in the garden at the front doing a bit of work. I sent him down to try and get him to stop moping around the house. I thought a bit of fresh air and activity would do him the power of good. Saoirse, I have to tell you I am fierce worried about him. He quit his job and is moping around here like the Mother of Sorrows all week. He is not eating great and by the look of him I don't think he is sleeping right either. I have never seen him like this before and I don't know what is eating him, but someone will have to get it out of him, and I hope you can. I think Padraig might have some idea, but he is a closed book, and you couldn't get anything out of him. Believe me, I am glad to see you, at least I know he will talk to you." "That's a lot of faith to put in me Geraldine." Haven't you been the best of friends for years? Do you know you are the best thing in his life, it's many a time I have said it to his Dad. Wouldn't you think that young fool Oisin would open his eyes and see what a fine girl you are? But that's neither here nor there now at the moment, I shouldn't be saying that to you either, I'm just so worried about him. Anyways I even called Padraig today to ask him if he would come out and have a word with him. Oisin always looked up to him, as a small lad and Padraig has a good head on his shoulders. To be honest I am worried that he is sick or something and that he can't bring himself to tell us." Christ, Saoirse thought, things must be bad if his mother was this upset. She usually took everything in her stride. It was also amazing that she had unknowingly put her finger on the issue. A mother's intuition Saoirse supposed. "Anyway Saoirse I have taken up enough of your time, he is down in the garden and you know where it is. Will you go down and see if you can talk some sense into him and get to the bottom of it? I will have some scones and tea here waiting for you when you get back."

Saoirse followed the path around the side of the house and opened the small red wooden gate into the garden. Oisin's mother's garden was a rather large, kitchen garden by any standards. It was walled by a dry-stone wall and was about 2 acres. It was beautiful, particularly in the evening sun. One wall was flanked by fruit bushes and trees including blueberries, gooseberries, raspberries, apple trees and strawberries in a raised bed. She used the fruit to make jams, jellies and juices, that she sold at the county market and to give to friends. The rest of the garden was planted with vegetables and a mixed planting of flowers. On opening the gate Saoirse could hear the clang of a shovel from the back of the garden, thinking he must not have received my text if he was still working away. She followed the sound of the noise along the winding garden path passing potatoes, onions and carrots that were just peeping over the ground. The carrots were covered with fleece to keep them warm from the night frost and to keep the green fly off them later in summer. The bees from the hive were buzzing about, adding a gentle background music to the whole scene. Walking through this beautiful tranquil place, she could see the attraction for Oisin in giving up work and taking over here full time. It really was truly idyllic; there was no comparison between sitting behind a desk in an office and working here. As she approached the back of the garden, she could see Oisin bending and straightening as he dug with the spade. There was something elemental in it. A man at one with nature, lost in his own world with an old collie dog relaxing on his jacket on the ground beside him. She paused and took in the scene not wanting to disturb man or beast. They were in harmony with their surroundings, oblivious to any intruder. Observing Oisin and with her new knowledge, she felt an awareness of his masculinity. The trickle of sweat dampening the back of his t-shirt from his exertions, his strong, powerful back muscles rippling under his t-shirt as he drove the shovel into the ground as if to exorcise some unseen demons from within. Standing there watching him she felt her heart flutter in her chest, and she knew instinctively this was her man. The man who loved her and, in that moment, she knew it was true for her as well. She loved him and in fact she acknowledged she always had.

She called his name and he nearly jumped out of his skin. As he turned to face her, she could see the ravages of the sleepless nights in the bags under his eyes and the strain on his face. He smiled at her, a shy sort of smile but he didn't say anything. Wow she thought, has it come to this? He seemed to have lost his voice and he certainly wasn't one to be lost for words. She walked up to him and put her arms around him for a hug. He wrapped his arms tightly around her and she could smell the sweat and earth off him. He rested his chin on top of her head and they just stood there in each other's arms without saying anything. After what seemed like an eternity, she lifted her head and looked him in the eye and said simply "I know" and "I do." He looked searchingly into her eyes and she could feel his body trembling as he bent over and kissed her lips. With a deep sigh, he said, "Thank God, I was terrified, I thought I had lost you." With tears in his eyes he simply said, "I love you Saoirse, I always have, and I always will." Time stood still as they just stood there wrapped in each other's arms, absorbing what had been said.

Eventually Saoirse said, "You know Oisin, I am still a bit in shock, but what I can't figure out is why you couldn't tell me?" "I just couldn't get the words out and hearing about you and him was eating me alive" he said. "Once I realised how I actually felt about you, I was terrified I would lose you. I was terrified you wouldn't feel the same. I knew if you didn't, I would lose my best friend as well because I wouldn't be able to continue as your friend, feeling the way I felt. I couldn't see you with another man, I just couldn't do it. She put her index finger to his lips and simply said "shush... it's ok." Shuddering he said "but Saoirse, I was terrified, and I couldn't do anything about it. I love you so much... I have never felt this way about anyone before. It scared me... "I am sorry Oisin" she said "really I am." "No need to be sorry Saoirse, it's mad, every time you mentioned your man, it was like a punch in the gut, and then when I saw you upset on Sunday it just tore me apart. I just couldn't figure out how to tell you and I was afraid I had lost you." "God Oisin, this is a lot to take in. I am glad, you got it out though, I really couldn't imagine my life without you in it either. But us as a couple is going to take a bit of getting used to." She closed her eyes and wrapped her arms around him and squeezed tight, resting her head on his chest and breathed him in. In that moment she realised that nothing had ever felt so right for her. It was like coming home. Never one to be quiet for too long Saoirse sighed, "Oisin, why has it taken us so long, all them years?" She lifted her head and looked up at him. He bent his head and kissed her in a deep possessive kiss, marking her as his own. Raising his head, he said, "I love you so much Saoirse, you wouldn't believe it, in fact I can hardly believe it myself. I now know why they have all the songs about how love hurts. I now truly understand." He stood back from her holding her at arm's length and with a smile in his eyes, for the first time looking a bit more like himself, said will you do me the honour and paused, she held her breath. "Will you do me the honour of cycling the Ring of Beara with me on Saturday?" She laughed and said, "I will and here was me thinking you were going to ask me to marry you." He laughed "We can get to that in the not too distant future, but for right now I would like to call you my girlfriend for a while." "God Saoirse" he said "when I think of all them wasted years, what were we playing at when we could have been together?" She looked at him and said, "Those years weren't wasted, we always had each other, we were growing up and learning about life. We weren't ready to make a commitment to each other or anyone else for that matter." "We were lucky though that neither of us made a commitment to anyone else" he said and he pulled her into his arms and kissed her again.

When she got her breath back, she said "Let's get out of here, do you want to come home with me?" His voice was shaking with emotion as he said, "I thought I would never hear you say them words." She said "Maybe we should go up and tell your mother that she will be one lodger less? I promised I would pop in on my way back from the garden." "I would love to skip it, and make a run for it with you, but I think she will be delighted and after having to put up with me for the past while it's the least I could do. I haven't actually been a joy to live with." Just as they came to the corner before they turned into the yard Oisin pulled her towards him and kissed her so tenderly and with such longing it brought tears to her eye, he whispered "I love you so much Saorise, I never want to let you go again" and he rubbed the tears gently from her eyes with his thumb. "I can't wait to be alone with you, to show you what you mean to me he whispered, but let's make my mother's day first."

His mother had been keeping an eye out from the kitchen window and when she saw them walking up hand in hand with big grins on their faces she made the sign of the cross and to herself said "not before time." She rushed out the door and gave them both a big hug and said, "What took ye so long, and I don't mean down in the garden today? … Oh Saoirse, you have made me a happy woman. I have been telling this git to open his eyes and see what he has with you, but it took him nearly losing you to figure it out. Anyways I am delighted; I must go and tell your father. But Christ lad, you gave me a right good scare this past week, you did. I was beginning to think we would be fishing you out of the lake if you kept going the way you were going. I must get your father. Now I am repeating myself, but I must get him and tell him the good news." "Hang on Mom awhile; we are not getting married just yet. Stop getting your knickers in a twist. Give us a chance to get used to this." "Ah lad, will you give over that nonsense, you love each other don't you, so what are ye waiting for, it's as simple as that. Life is too short, and it's not like ye just met. Do you know what, this, calls for a garden party. I am going to have one early next week. That should give me enough time to get everything done and make sure everyone is here." Oisin knew when he was beat, if his mother had made up her mind, she was having a garden party, then she was, so there was no point in fighting it. "That would be lovely Mom" he said. "Now I am going to tell your father" she said for the third time. "Will ye be here when we get back?" Oisin knew it was now or never to get out or there would be no escape for the evening. "No Mom I am going to gather my things and head back with Saoirse." "Right so" she said "have a great evening, don't do anything I wouldn't do and she winked at him. I couldn't be happier for the two of you" and she gave Saoirse another rib cracking hug, before bolting out the door calling his father's name.

Oisin turned to Saoirse gave her a quick kiss and said, "Wait here, I will run upstairs and grab my bits before she comes back." Without waiting for an answer, he bolted up the stairs taking them two at a time. Within about two minutes flat he was back down with a bag thrown over his shoulder and declared, "let's get out of here." They jumped into the car and tore out of the driveway like someone in a high speed chase. Saoirse covered the distance between Oisin's parents' place and hers in record time. Just before they pulled up to the door Oisin reached over and took her hand and smiled, and simply said "to us." "To us," she replied.

Stepping out of the car Saoirse suddenly felt nervous, it dawned on her that this was real and happening, the next chapter of her life had begun. No more would they be just friends; they were now a couple and their lives would be forever changed. There was no going back here. As she opened the door, she found herself trembling. They had come through this door so many times as friends, but this time was different. It wouldn't be her front door anymore it would be their front door. She knew in her heart that nothing or no one had ever been so right for her. She reached back behind her for his hand and led him through the house to her bedroom. The only room in the house he had been excluded from before. It had always been her room and hers alone. She had never brought another man in here. Bringing him through her bedroom door she was offering to share her space and her life with him. There and then she decided that she was going to make this moment, one they would always remember.

In silence, she left his hand go, walked to the window, closed the curtains, and turned on the old-fashioned CD player on her nightstand from which a beautiful haunting piano melody played. Turning around she glided to the middle of the room where, moving slowly and hypnotically to the music, she began to undress. He was transfixed to the spot as she slowly and languidly removed her t- shirt to reveal her small pert breasts enclosed in a black lace bra that was aching to be caressed, she shimmied out of her trousers and kicked them to the side revealing a matching black wisp of lace covering her female secrets. Swaying rhythmically to the music she locked eyes with him and reached both arms overhead and loosened her hair letting it float over her shoulders. She then began to peel her bra off one shoulder at a time, displaying pert breasts with nipples standing to attention. He saw the final black slip of fabric float to the ground revealing her full beauty. As she began to move towards him, he released his breath that he hadn't realised he was holding. She took the bottom of his t-shirt and lifted it over his head while allowing her nipples to tease his chest. With a groan he wrapped his hands in her hair and tried to capture her mouth as she dropped his pants to reveal his hard, appreciative erection. Placing her hand on his chest she backed him backwards until he was seated on the edge of her bed, with one fluid movement she straddled him, and with confident hands, rolled a condom the full length of his erect penis. Looking in his eyes she asked “do you want to do this?” “Of course,” he moaned. Closing the gap between them she took him deep inside her while his arms came round her waist securing her at full depth. She lifted his chin in both hands and made love to his face in tender kisses tracing her lips over that familiar mouth, nose and eyes while slowly moving her hips and building their passion. His lips followed the curve of her jaw and ran down her neck as she arched her back taking him deeper inside her. Continuing on his journey of exploration he travelled from neck to shoulder to breast where with his tongue he took her nipple in his mouth and massaging her free breast with his hand he sucked until she was totally lost and riding with abandon. Together they crested the wave collapsing in each other’s arms on release.

They lay like that for a time. Oisin’s mind utterly blown; never in his wildest dreams did he think it would be like that with Saoirse. Over the years he couldn’t count the number of women he had slept with, but it had never been like this. With Saoirse it was fierce and beautiful and almost spiritual. She had totally and utterly given herself to him. As he looked down at her relaxing in the afterglow, he felt a fierce need to cherish and protect her. “Thank you, Saoirse” he whispered, “I love you with all my heart.” He then began to kiss her tenderly, gently expressing his love for her in each touch. He let his free arm glide up and down her beautiful slender, taut body, gradually moving towards her breasts, circling her erect nipples between fore finger and thumb, gently rolling them, sending waves of pleasure through her body. At his touch she sighed, and her body softened and opened giving free access to his touch. He traced his finger down between her breasts, following a pathway over her navel, playing gently for a moment in her pubic hair and then sliding it between her legs and into her warm moist and waiting vagina. He slowly and rhythmically began the dip and slide with his finger over her clitoris, sending waves of pleasure through her. Joining with his mouth, he made love to her with his tongue and finger in rhythmic unison until she was begging for more. Covering his erect penis with a condom, he slid home into her open wetness. Wrapping her legs around his back, she opened up, taking his swollen penis to its full depth, locking them both together. With a deep-throated moan, he was lost, his brain blank to anything other than the sheer pleasure of passion as he plunged rhythmically into Saoirse, consummating their years of friendship and love.

After a while Saoirse said, "I don't know about you Oisin, but I need a drink and something to eat. How would scrambled eggs and toast sound for afternoon tea?" He laughed, sat up and said, "Let's do it. I will make the tea and toast, you do the eggs." "Deal" she said. Pulling on some clothes, they both went down to the kitchen for a bite to eat. As they were putting the food on the table, he took both her hands in his and turned her towards him, and looking her in the eye, he said. "Saoirse, I know this is a bit premature, but I am in love with you, in fact I now realise I always have been in love with you. After this past week I know there is no one else for me but you. I would like to spend the rest of my life with you, raise our children together, and grow old together. Bottom line is, I love you, getting down on one knee right there by her kitchen table he said Saoirse, Mary Murphy will you marry me?" With tears in her eyes she replied "Oh! Oisin, of course I will. I love you with all my heart. I would love to spend the rest of my life with you." "Let's raise a mug of tea to that" he joked. They raised their mugs of tea and toasted, "to a healthy, happy and fun future together."

Saoirse said "let's eat now and start our planning for the future." On one thing though, she said, "I think maybe we should wait a little while longer for the children. I would like to have some more afternoons like we just had with only the two of us." He lifted the palm of her hand and kissing it said "Amen to that.

We can go into town tomorrow and look for the ring and maybe we can make an announcement at my mother's garden party the next week." "We also have another Ring to prepare for on Saturday week. Do you still want to cycle the Ring of Beara, or with all this excitement do you want to give it a miss, this year?" "Absolutely not, we will have to do it. Which one did you sign up for?" "The short one," she replied, "I didn't feel like taking on the hills in around

Allihies, although I will miss the beach food stop as that is spectacular, nothing like it on any other cycle, but I don't think I could put myself through them hills." "Yeah I know he said, to be honest I have signed up for the 140km but I think I would prefer to have a nice leisurely day out with my new fiancée." "Oh Oisin, will you say that again" she whispered. "That I would like the leisurely day out," he teased. "No, you daft fool, the part about with your fiancée" she cried.

Whatever way she looked out the window she noticed someone striding towards her door. "Oh shit," she muttered, "this is not good timing." Getting up from the table, she headed for the door. Oisin hadn't seen him so he jokingly said, "What have I done? Why are you leaving me in such a hurry already? Over her shoulder she called, "Donal is outside, I am going to see what he wants." "Jesus Christ that lad doesn't give up easy, does he?" Oisin said as he followed her into the hallway. As Donal approached the door Saoirse opened it. He was delighted to see her. He had expected to be kept on the doorstep for awhile, in his head he had played out several scenarios including pleading through the letterbox. Maybe... just maybe she has forgiven me he thought. This might not be too bad he thought to himself again in silent reassurance.

CHAPTER 14

If we truly love someone, we have to accept them flaws and all

He smiled his winning smile, hoping to ease the tension that he sensed in her immediately. She only glared at him and asked, "what are you doing here?" "That's a nice welcome isn't it," he replied. Looking around he said, "You have a lovely place here, can I come in?" "No, you can't, and by the way, how did you find my place? I am nearly certain I didn't give you my address. How did you find me?" Then it dawned on her that he already knew where she lived. Hadn't he sent her a bunch of flowers already. At that thought she got a shiver down her spine. "Well … how did you find me?" "Look it doesn't matter how I found you" Donal replied. "I just wanted to see you again. I wanted … to check that you were alright and … and to see you again." "I thought I made myself clear when I was leaving that we were done, it's a bit stalkerish to just turn up on my doorstep don't you think?" Oisin, having been listening to the exchange in the hallway, chose this moment to make his appearance. He slung his arm proprietarily over Saoirse's shoulder saying, "Everything all right here Si?" Donal noticed the look of protection and possession in Oisin's eyes and body language. Wow, Donal thought to himself, it looks like things here have taken a turn in a different direction. "Yes, I just called around to Saoirse to check to see if she was all right," Donal said. Addressing Saoirse, he said "I just wanted to see how you got on Monday, I was really worried about you, you know."

So that's it she thought, he is wondering if I went to the doctor and looked after things. "You have some bloody cheek" Oisin said ominously, "after the state you left her in on Sunday, to just rock up here uninvited." Shrugging off his arm and taking hold of his hand, Saoirse exclaimed, "For God's sake Oisin, will you give him a chance to get a word out, there was two of us in it you know." Oisin winced at that. He didn't want to think of her involvement in it. Taking the situation in hand Saoirse said, "Right, inside the both of you, I am not having this conversation on the doorstep." Noticing that the two lads were still sizing each other up, she said "enough, we are going to act like adults here or you can both get out." With the ground rules set, she pushed past Oisin, who was still silently challenging Donal to enter. "If you are sure Saoirse," Donal said. She turned around and said "just come inside, the two of you."

Once in the kitchen she said to Donal: "I am sorry if you came here today hoping to get back together, that is not going to happen. To answer your earlier question on Monday, I went to the doctor and got an STI test." The two men winced at her bluntness. "I don't have the full results yet, so I am awaiting them." "OK" Donal said nervously, "I don't think you will have anything to worry about from them. I don't make a habit of it..... you know, despite what you might think of me." She could sense that Oisin was absolutely fuming beside her. She was beginning to wonder if he could resist throwing a punch in defence of her non-existent honour. She was fed up of all this male testosterone. She turned to him and said "Oisin if you would like to leave for this conversation you are welcome, I can handle it myself." He laughed contemptuously, but reaching out he took her hand and, looking Donal in the eye, said " We are planning on getting married, we don't want to start by keeping secrets, do we? It is just as good hearing it all now as later." Saoirse was a little startled by that response, there seemed to be an edge of a threat in it, but she carried on. This conversation needed to be had.

Donal knew he had, at the very least, lost Saoirse, but he thought he might as well see how far he could push Oisin. He knew he was like a rocket ready to explode. He would do a bit of stirring of his own. 'Saoirse if you don't mind me asking, did you take care of the other situation?" She spun on him saying "What sort of a question is that?" "All I'm asking is did you get the emergency contraception, since Oisin here appears to be prepared to marry you, I am sure he would want to know if you are carrying my child or not." "Ah fuck off," Oisin roared, "get out of here before I burst you open you, bollocks." Donal stood his ground, he was not one to scare easily, he was after all a master of the boardroom and things could get nasty in there too. "Simple question Saoirse, did you get the emergency contraception or not?" Donal persisted.

Oisin was barely containing himself at this point, but he knew that if he laid a hand on Donal, Saoirse was capable of asking him to leave. He also knew that was what Donal was angling for. Both men turned towards Saoirse waiting for her answer. Holding both her hands up she said, "I did not." "Jesus Christ Saoirse ...What are you playing at? Do you mean you could actually be pregnant and by him?" Oisin asked, nodding violently at Donal. "Would it matter Oisin if I was?" She replied in a hurt tone. Donal couldn't believe this drama, he found himself holding his breath as he waited for Oisin to answer. "Saoirse you know I love you, so I suppose it wouldn't matter" he said unconvincingly. Saoirse, looking disappointed, said "It's most unlikely that I am ... Sunday was 3 weeks since my last period, if ye both must know, I have exercise-induced amenorrhea. With all the cycling and exercise, my periods are very irregular so I couldn't be sure." The two lads looked at each other and, despite their animosity for each other, both their male looks said too much information. "So now lads, we have to wait, as I have no intention of putting a dose of hormones into my body … I am going to let nature take its course and see what happens." "Right of course" Donal began, "it's your body.... I respect your choice." Oisin was fuming, Donal had all the answers, he couldn't even speak, he couldn't believe how stupid and stubborn she was. "Saoirse," Donal said "if it's OK with you, I will leave now, you know where to find me if you need me." He turned to Oisin saying, "I wish you both the best of luck, but if she is carrying my child, rest assured, I will be its father." Oisin was dumbstruck, how could you answer that? If he accepted it, he was accepting the fact there was going to be three of them in the relationship. But if he wanted to be with Saoirse had he any choice? He wondered who would be the third wheel in this relationship, him or Donal?

Oisin was gobsmacked by the fact that Saoirse had made a conscious decision to have a child. Yes, he knew it hadn't been planned, but hadn't they just been talking about having children earlier this morning and she said she wanted to wait until they had some time together. God, he thought, women were confusing. Now she was saying although that while it was unlikely, she could be pregnant. He was totally confused. God forbid if she actually had the child, it would be a constant reminder of Donal for the rest of their life together. He acknowledged he had a choice here. To be with the love of his life or let her go. This was the crossroads he was on, he would have to make a choice and live with the consequences.

He knew he had to get a bit of perspective here and fast. If presented with this situation, what would Padraig say? Oisin immediately knew Padraig would say something like 'grow a pair, life is not straightforward, either deal with it or walk away'. Oisin was aware that Saoirse loved him and he acknowledged that he loved her beyond all doubt, but could he share her? He was man enough to recognise also that he had made a few mistakes himself in his time, but the women involved had always sorted it out. He knew he had to stop thinking of it as a mistake. This was a child he was talking about. A little person that deserved to be loved by all the adults in its life. He also knew that if, Saoirse had a child she would put it before any man. The question was though, was he man enough to accept her and the situation as it was and not as he had planned? He decided that the best course of action was to make no decision and see what would happen in the coming weeks. He could only hope …

Taking Saoirse's hand, he said, "Saoirse, I love you, as I said earlier, there can be no topics off limits if we are to make this work." "Are you sure?" she asked as she looked at him with tears in her eyes. "Oisin, what happens if I am pregnant? I will not change my mind; I am going to take my chance on nature.... Can you accept that, or are we finished?" "Saoirse I will admit, it hurts, but I do love you, this situation.... will take a bit of getting used to, but I want to be with you." She leaned into him and kissed him. "Thank you Oisin, I really do love you." "I know" he said "but you do realise if you are pregnant, there will be three of us in this relationship. You said yourself he was mad for a wife and children, but even if he doesn't get the wife, he will not give up his child. You heard him."

CHAPTER 15

Life happens, we cannot control it, but we can roll with it

On leaving Saoirse's house Donal felt a bit deflated. He had hoped to charm her after her initial and fully expected outburst. He had not bargained for Oisin being there too, nor for them to have gotten together. That seemed bizarre to him, what could have pushed them to such a solid commitment after all this time? Oisin had intimated that they were getting married. That all seemed a bit fast to him as it was only Thursday. He had slept with Saoirse on Saturday night and what they had shared Sunday morning, before the 'situation', was special. At the time she definitely was not thinking of getting married to someone else. He couldn't figure out what could have happened in the mean time to push them together. He laughed sardonically as he remembered Oisin's face when Saoirse started going on about an STI test and not doing a pregnancy test. Oisin had been beside himself. Now there's a man who would never make a poker player Donal thought, you could read his face like a book.

It was not how Donal had envisioned becoming a father, but he knew that if by chance Saoirse was pregnant and that child was his, no one would keep him away from it. He knew that despite Saoirse's hot-headedness, she would do whatever she felt was best for their child. He felt that Oisin would also be a good father-figure once he came to terms with it. He decided that, to be on the safe side, he would research custody and paternity testing tonight. He knew he had very few rights because they were not married, but he would do whatever it took to be in his child's life.

Saoirse felt that taking a pregnancy test was what she needed to do? She had to find out if she was pregnant or not. After her little bit of research on the internet she knew this wouldn't be easy for her with her irregular periods. To do an effective test, a lot of what she had read said to wait until your period was late, but how was she to know when her's was? In the past year she had only had about five and there was no pattern. Recently she had been doing a lot of training, so it was going to be difficult to tell when her's was due. She also knew that, despite all the anguish both Oisin and Donal were going through, it was highly unlikely that she would be pregnant. She felt annoyed with both of them. They had pushed her into answering that question. She acknowledged that both of them would make good dads in different ways and it wouldn't be so bad even if it was a little complicated to rear a child between three of them. They would both just have to grow up and stop treating her like a possession to fight over. She would be threading a fine balance for awhile, but they would accept it in time she felt. She hadn't realised Oisin would be so jealous and she also still hadn't figured out how Donal had found her address. It unnerved her a little that he had been able to find her so easy. She decided that she would give herself three more weeks and then she would take the test if her period hadn't arrived. She knew it would be difficult to wait but she calculated that if by then she was pregnant something hormonal would have happened that would show up on the test.

On the morning of the Ring of Beara cycle Saoirse woke with a dull ache in her back, which told her motherhood was not to be this time. Mother nature had decided the timing was not right. Saoirse couldn't believe the disappointment. In her own mind she had planned her little family. She had accepted the two men in her life. She knew Oisin would be thrilled with the news that she wasn't pregnant and that hurt deeply. She had hoped he would have accepted her situation as time passed because he loved her, but he had been unable to. For all he had said about being there for her and loving her she had felt him emotionally withdraw as the week passed. She had also seen him, watching her for signs. When they made love last night in some way, she had felt the connection was not there. She wondered if they could come back from this.

As she came out of the bathroom having confirmed what her back ache already told her, Oisin walked in and sensing her mood asked, "Saoirse are you alright, you don't look so well?" She smiled weakly at him and climbed back into the bed. That made him really look at her. Today was the cycle and she should have been skipping out the door. She didn't look like she was going anywhere. He asked again, "What's wrong, are you feeling sick?" She shook her head and started to cry. He was over to the bed to her in an instant. "What is it Saoirse, love?" he asked. Between sobs she got out, "I'm not .... I'm not pregnant." He was at a loss; he didn't know how to respond. Inside he was jumping for joy, but he could see she was devastated. He couldn't believe her reaction. Surely this had to be a good thing for the two of them. They could get on with their lives now as they had planned. "Saoirse" he said taking her hand gently, "I don't understand. Did you really want to have his baby." That did it, turning away, she said "If you think that you really haven't a clue. It's all about him for you. This was my baby, my chance to be a mother. It wasn't about him or you for me." He climbed into the bed and cradled her saying, "Saoirse I am sorry, I'm a man, as you say, I just don't understand. All I know is I love you." While he spoke, he stroked her hair and kissed the back of her neck. "I do want to have children with you, but I want them to be.... ours."

She turned and smiled at him weakly. "I'm sorry Oisin. I am all over the place, I loved the idea of being pregnant...." "I know you did Saoirse." "Maybe it's my age, but once I got the idea into my head that I was about to be a mother that's all I wanted." He pulled her gently to him and said, "Well, if you want to give it another go I would be happy to oblige." At that she gave him a punch and said even with your best efforts this morning it wouldn't happen today. He pulled her into his arms and said, "Saoirse I love you, we have the rest of our lives to become parents and it will be our decision." "I know" she said "but for today lets, do this cycle. It will be fun and we both could do with some fresh air and the open road."

Riding out of Kenmare with Oisin by her side, Saoirse felt some of the weight lift off her shoulders. Her mind began to clear with the exercise, fresh air and the fact that she now had a goal and some direction. Yes, she still felt a little sad, because in her mind she had already been planning for a life with her child. She acknowledged though, in truth, this did seem like the better option for her. She and Oisin could now at least plan for their future without the complication of Donal in their lives too. She knew what she wanted in life now, she now had a meaningful goal worth striving for again. It's amazing she thought, how life just happens, and it can totally change one's focus. Her priorities in life had been reset in such a short time, literally over the past few days. She knew in her heart that this would probably be her final big ride for a while. If she wanted to be a mom, she would have to put the long-distance cycling on hold. For the past few years, she had been freewheeling through life, but now she had a goal. She wanted to be a mom. She wanted it more than a wedding and a lot more than cycling. She vowed to enjoy today though, for what it was. A celebration of years of training, of volunteerism and 4,000 cyclists each with their individual hopes and dreams.

She felt lucky to be alive as she rode along with Oisin by the estuary out of Kenmare. It was a beautiful sunny morning; she noted the fresh air and exercise seemed to be doing him good also. He had visibly relaxed in himself. Coming over from Killarney in the car he had still been edgy. It was like he didn't know what to say to her. He didn't seem to know how to be around her anymore. She acknowledged that the last two weeks had been rocky, they had been a massive strain on both of them. What should have been the best two weeks of their lives, was probably the most difficult they had ever shared.

As they began to head into the hills on the way from Lauragh she decided to have the tough conversation with him. She realised that they had their full lives ahead of them, but she really and truly wanted to clear the air. On the bike was a great place to have a conversation. Even with thousands on the road at this point there was only the two of them. She knew he would have no escape. "Oisin" she began "I am really sorry for all I put you through over the past two weeks, I know it wasn't easy." "Saoirse it's OK, the main thing is we have come through it. I must admit at times I wondered if we would." "In truth Oisin I did too." "While I knew you loved me Saoirse, if you were pregnant with his child he would be forever in our lives. I found it really difficult to see beyond that." "I know Oisin … I know I underestimated the complexity of the situation, particularly as we really are only starting out as a couple. I think now though, we can move on.... can't we?" she asked hopefully. He smiled and momentarily reached out his hand to hers. "Of course, we can. Knowing you though", he joked to lighten the mood "you will want to start trying straight away. You got a taste for motherhood now." Little did he know he had actually nailed the purpose of her conversation.

She smiled and said, "You are right there. Would you be happy to push out the wedding a year or two and give it a go?" He laughed, then looking at her, he wobbled on the bike saying, "Jesus Saoirse you're not joking, are you? Look Saoirse … whatever you want I am happy to go with you. I am after nearly losing you twice and I don't think I could stand another round of it." "I would like to try" she said wistfully "but it might take time. I will have to take a step back from the training and let my body get ready." " You have given this serious thought so have you Saoirse?"

"Of course, Oisin, why do you think I wasn't talking to you on the way out of Kenmare?" "Christ who knows" he began"here was I thinking you were just enjoying the peace and quiet. If I had realised you were plotting my future, I would have interrupted you," he joked.

With that he changed the conversation to the trivialities of the ride. She knew that, as far as he was concerned for now, the conversation was closed, and she accepted that. As they approached Ardgroom there was bikes everywhere. Trying to get a spot to park theirs was nearly impossible. They eventually found a spot and in their new found happiness really settled into the fun of the day, sharing in the banter with the other cyclists and queuing for the coffee and the customary sandwiches and bars. They had made a pact that they would stop everywhere today and just enjoy the day and each others company. They were in no hurry.

CHAPTER 16

Making plans and anticipating their outcome is one of life's simple pleasures

Heading uphill from Ardgroom the views were amazing. On their right they had Kenmare bay and the mountains to their left. "Just look at that" Saoirse said, pointing out the little fishing boat going about its business with the sun glistening on the flat, calm sea. "Images like that are why we do this aren't they?" "I suppose" Oisin said. "But I like to think it's for the challenge and because we can." They continued in contemplative silence as the road swung gently upwards passing a quarry, before heading downhill to Eyeries. As they reached the GAA pitch in Eyeries, Saoirse turned to Oisin saying, "decision time, are we taking this handy or are we heading for Allihies?" "I don't know Saoirse it's up to you … Allihies is absolutely stunning but them mountains literally rise out of the sea. After that house in the middle of the road the hills literally turn into beasts and it feels like they are never going to end, it's one hill after another. It's absolutely stunning though, so it's up to you. What do you want to do?" "You know what,' Saoirse began. "I'm enjoying today, it's early enough in the season, let's just take it handy and do the short one, that's what I signed up for anyways."

With that they continued on for Castletownbere and the main food stop. As they pedalled along Oisin said, "You know, we really need to have a chat about the wedding, like when and where and all that. Also, there is really one important conversation we need to have." "What's that?" "Your mother." "What about my mother?" Saoirse replied. "Sure, she can't stand me, or my rough crowd as she calls us. I don't think she ever saw me as potential husband material for you, her darling daughter." "I don't think I really am that much of a 'darling', I am too much of a tomboy, she can't stand this cycling you know." "I know and who will she blame for that?" Oisin replied. "I know your Dad will be fine about it," he continued, "we got on well doing the house, but your mom, now she's a different story."

"I know" Saoirse laughed. "Do you remember the day you broke the back kitchen window, that was the last time you were left in the door at our place wasn't it?" "I will never forget that day" he laughed. "It was some craic, she was raging, I thought she was going to take the rolling pin to me or something." "You were lucky she didn't" Saoirse giggled. "I know" he laughed "I can still see it, all we were doing was having a kick around, when I booted a hard one at Sean, he missed, and it went straight through the kitchen window." "God Oisin, I can still hear the sound, there was glass everywhere. I think it was more the fright of it than anything, but she was raging, wasn't she?" "Do you remember what she said to me?" he asked. "'Get out of here you good for nothing thug you, and stay away from my daughter, she said while shaking the rolling pin at me. I tell you, I moved quick that day." "Well" Saoirse began," I am not telling them on my own, so you are going to have to come with me. I think we should do it this evening when we get back and get it over with." "I suppose so, what do you think of them coming to mom's garden party for the engagement?" "I don't know," Saoirse replied, "I think Dad and Sean would enjoy one of your mother's parties but I'm not sure about Mom. If it gets a bit rough, she will only be worried about the wedding for the whole time." "Maybe we would be better to keep the two families separate until the day of the wedding," he suggested. "First things first though, we had better break the news to them before they hear it from anywhere else", she said

"By the way, when do you think we should get married? I think I would like a Christmas wedding myself," Saoirse mused aloud, "although a summer wedding in your mother's garden would also be nice too." "You might be on to something there with the garden … We could get a marquee or do up the barn, you know the one near the garden? You know if we did up the barn, we might be able to use it as a farm shop afterwards to sell some of our produce. What do you think?" Oisin asked Saoirse excitedly, but he carried on dreaming without waiting for her to reply. "You know Saoirse, I'm planning to extend our produce and this might really work out. It's dual function, a wedding venue and a shop, it's genius Saoirse. We wouldn't be wasting any money on a hotel venue, but we would have a good structure afterwards that we could use."

She felt a little disappointed that he was looking at their wedding in such monetary terms, but she could see his reasoning made sense. Trying to set up a new business and have a wedding at the same time would be expensive. If one could help out the other then it made sense, it was just so unromantic. She couldn't help but feel a little sorry to lose her dream of a big white wedding in a fancy hotel at Christmas. In her heart she would love the romance of that, but she would accept a summer wedding in the barn, if it could speed up the wedding. Now that she had a taste for motherhood, she wanted to pursue that dream without too much delay. If they could organise the barn wedding in a few months she would settle for that. She knew her mother would go absolutely mental when she heard these plans. She could imagine it, she would be straight on the phone to her sister Mary saying, "My daughter is getting married in a shed, a shed, can you imagine that? You know he doesn't even have a proper job now, he jacked it in you know, to go gardening, how are they going to manage on that?" She could just hear it already. By God she thought to herself, Oisin is definitely coming with me to break all this news.

"It would certainly be different," she said to Oisin, "I am happy to go with your mother's garden and the barn, but the question remains as to when? Do we wait until next year or could we manage it in September?" "I don't know, we are in May now so that would give us 4 months. We probably could pull it off if we could get a licence. We would have to skip the cycling and what about your plans to have a baby?"

Saoirse was quiet for a while thinking about it until she said finally, "I think we should just go for it, if we can. We can put off the baby stuff for a few months anyways, which gives my body a chance to settle itself, if I cut back on the exercise." "I think it's 3 months notice you have to give but we can check that out. I think we should just go for it, if your willing." "As your Mom would say, what are we waiting for? Let's do it, a September wedding, it's not like we don't know each other and we don't have to have some completely mad outrageous affair." Reaching out to him on the bike, she momentarily touched his arm and said, "You know Ois, you're right, let's do it …" "I can see it already" he said, "we will have the ceremony in a marquee down by the river, followed by the reception in the barn. We can then clear away the tables and have a barn dance afterwards, what do you think?" "I think it's a mighty idea," she chuckled, "let's get some county rock singer to do the music and it will be a right shindig." "I can just see it, me spinning you around the floor to some really good country rock, hay bales as seats and lanterns overhead, it would be some craic for a wedding" he said excitedly. "Once today is over we will have to get cracking on this..."

"I know Oisin, we need to start with a list and work from there, book the ceremony, the marquee, caterers, singer, photographer, and of course the builders to get started with the barn … First though we better check with your parents to see if they will let us have it at yours." "God Saoirse, that's a lot of work over …" She blew him a kiss and said, in her best American drawl, "Honey, y'all know dreams take work to make them happen … but I am with you 100% of the way. I do draw the line though on jeans and shirts as the dress code for the ceremony." "Maybe we should just have the family for dinner and everyone else for the barn dance", he said. "Now you're talking Oisin, it would be less pressure and they could wear their jeans and shirts to that if they liked?" "Now all we have to do is convince your mother this is a good idea and run it past mine. We will have to start this evening you know, I will talk to my mom, then we can call over to yours, no point in putting that off any longer," he stated.

As they were coming down the hill into Castletownbere the music blasting from the loud-speakers brought them back to the present. Hundreds of bikes were already racked in the square. Picnic tables had been set up to feed the cyclists with free food supplied to everyone participating. The atmosphere was electric, the pubs and cafes were also doing a roaring trade feeding all the cyclists' families and supporters. People were milling around everywhere. Random groups of strangers were all seated together at the picnic benches fuelling themselves for the road ahead. Conversations were easy because they all had the cycle in common. There were clubs from all over the country mixed through with individuals and groups of friends out for the day.

As Saoirse was looking around for a free space at a table, her eyes were drawn to one cyclist in a group coming in off the 140km cycle. She would recognise him anywhere. With a jolt she thought, he does look good on a bike, but I was really hoping not to have to deal with him today. Giving Oisin a dig in the ribs she said, "look over there, just coming into the square from the Allihies side." Oisin turned and looked but all he could see was a group of lads coming in, nothing special in that. "Who is it?" he asked, "I can't tell with the helmets from here." He could feel that Saoirse had tensed up beside him, but he had no idea who it was. "What will I do?" she asked. "How do you mean, what will you do?" replied Oisin, and he didn't know what had gotten into her. "I don't really want to face him right now." "Saoirse, who is it? It's not like you to be running from someone." "It's Donal you big eejit.. "Never mind him, we will find an end of a table and sit down and eat our sandwiches and drink our tea. He probably won't come near us anyways. He would have a hard job to find you here in the middle of all this" he said, spreading his hands indicating the amount of people milling around. "Come on" Oisin said, as he took her free hand in his and guided her to a table near them.

Saoirse couldn't believe it when, just as they were settling in at the table having their cup of tea, Donal appeared. "Well how's it going, fabulous day?" he said. "Which one did ye do?" he asked after neither Oisin or Saoirse replied to his first question. "Ah the short one" Saoise replied eventually "What about you?" "The 140km, Allihies was stunning. The stop was at the beach this year. A couple of us even stuck our legs in the water, you wouldn't believe the effect on the calves." "I thought you were allergic to the beach" "Ah you know, it was only a quick dip, we weren't there all day" "Oh right, ye flew over that massive climb, from the beach so?" Saoirse asked as she reflected to herself how awkward the whole thing was. "We did" Donal began, … come to think of it Saoirse, should you really be here today in your condition?" Looking at Oisin, he said "I would have thought you would be taking better care of her than this?" "Ah fuck off", Oisin said, rising to the bait, "what Saoirse does is none of your business." "Are you sure of that?" Donal asked Oisin knowingly. Saoirse meanwhile was getting really annoyed with this exchange. Turning on Donal between gritted teeth she said "for your information, I am not pregnant, nor was I, so you are going to have to get over all this and leave me alone." "How can I be sure of that?" "Jesus Christ Donal you are just going to have to trust me unless you want to come to the bathroom, and I can show you." "No need to be crude, I don't think we need to go that far " he replied. "Good because as far as I am concerned", she said "this is case closed, I am done with this topic. It was a mistake and that is that. I am moving on. If I have to have this conversation with you again, I will file for harassment and that is that." "Such a pity," Donal continued, just to annoy Oisin, "we had some serious fun together, if we had made a baby it would have been born of desire." At that Oisin said, "come on Saoirse we don't have to listen to any more of his crap." Up they got leaving Donal standing there.

Donal knew he had gone too far with that one, but he couldn't help pushing Oisin's buttons. It was so easy. He had looked him up online and from the reports on the games he had played in the club championship, he could see he always was a hot head. It had looked like he had had a promising career in the GAA if he could have kept his temper in check. From what Donal had read he seemed to get yellow cards regularly and had a couple of red cards to his name too. He could see why, he rose to the bait easily.

Donal had already conceded it was over between himself and Saoirse for now. The fact she wasn't pregnant seemed to Donal to end even the slightest chance he had of getting back together with her in the immediate future. It was a pity, but he would have to leave her go, and see how she got on with Oisin. While he had conceded defeat in this round, he would keep an eye from a distance and see what happened. Oisin with his hot head would not be the easiest to live with. How would he be if they had a bad season on the farm or maybe a couple of them, or what if, as Saoirse had implied with the amenorrhoea business, they had difficulty having children. Would Oisin manage to keep his head? Donal also wondered if Saoirse would be cut out for the role of the farmer's wife. As far as he could tell she had no real experience of what it was like to try and make a living off the land. How would she be if she found herself working to fund a business that would take years to build and would eat money in the process. He wondered could her head be turned by the finer things in life if she had to endure some hardship first. He acknowledged to himself that in many of his best deals in business he had played the long game and it had paid off for him. Yeah, I can wait this one out for a while and see what happens, Donal thought to himself. She would have made an amazing wife and he knew she also would make a great mother. There was just something about her. He still felt there was a bit of a spark between them, but Oisin was in the way.

As Saoirse and Oisin headed out past Dinish Island, Oisin said, "You know Saoirse you would want to be careful with him. I think he may have a bit of a screw loose. He seems to have some stalker tendencies." "Ah Oisin I don't know, I think he just really enjoys winding you up as well as being a sore loser. I don't think he likes the fact that we are together. I think in his head, he and I were married the night I stayed over. I think he is desperate for a wife and children and he had me written into that role. I think he is harmless enough though." "Well I don't like him, I think he is a bit of a creep" Oisin said in a bit of a huff. "I don't think so," she replied, "deep down I think he is one of the good guys, if maybe a little socially challenged." "We will see" Oisin replied.

Saoirse loved this part of the cycle. On her right was beautiful Bere Island. An inhabited island home to a military barracks on one end of the island and a decommissioned lighthouse on the other. They had visited it a few years back while staying in the Berehaven Lodge. As they passed the Lodge she said,"Oisin do you remember the weekend we stayed there?" "Don't remind me, wasn't that the place we stayed in when I nearly lost you in the fog up on Hungry Hill." "God yeah" she said "don't remind me of that, it was one tough climb. I was thinking more of the amazing sea food, and the view over the bay from their dining room. It was fabulous. You know I was hoping back then that we would get together." "Were you? I never copped it." "I really thought it might happen back then," she said wistfully. "After that weekend I gave up on us, ever being anything more than friends, you know."

CHAPTER 17

What we imagine to be true, may often just be that, our imagination

They meandered away shooting the breeze with other cyclists as they passed until they got to that slow tedious pull from Adrigole. As they were grinding out the hill for a distraction Saoirse said, "I never even asked you how did you get your mother to defer the garden party by the way?" "I just told her you were sick" he said, "and that you wouldn't be up for a big shindig. Sure, she couldn't go ahead with it without both of the guests of honour present, could she?" "I suppose not, she must have been annoyed though" Saoirse said. "Yerrah, she got over it, anyways, there was no way I was up to their interrogation when we had all that hanging over us. As soon as they laid eyes on us, they would have known something was up. Whatever about you, I couldn't have faced them" he said. "Then we had this on this weekend, so she agreed to defer it until next weekend. Apparently, this is going to be her best one yet, she had invited all the aunties and the cousins as well. "She did not" Saoirse replied. "She did.

Mom said she is really celebrating now that she is going to see me up the aisle too. I think she had given up hope on me, you know. Also, I think you are actually her favourite of all the daughter in laws." Saoirse laughed. "It's funny a few weeks ago I was only wondering if I would be invited to the annual garden party, now I am actually guest of honour. It's amazing really how life works out."

Saoirse gritted her teeth as she ground out the last of the hill. She knew it would be worth it once they got to the top. They would practically be able to freewheel from there to Glengarriff. The scenery would be breathtaking, Bantry Bay with Whiddy Island in the distance and Garnish island closer to Glengarriff. Garnish island would just appear as they rounded a corner. She was looking forward to seeing it's majestic big trees and tiny inlets. With the gulf stream for warmth, Garnish island she knew is home to a beautiful tropical garden and the largest common seal colony in Ireland.

Saoirse and Oisin took a quick pit stop in Glengarriff and headed on for the final leg of the journey back to Kenmare. They couldn't really celebrate, until they got to the top of the Caha Pass, an 8km steady climb from bottom to top. Keeping the pace slow and steady they headed for the top, up past the nature reserve and on upwards with the sheer drops from the side of the road down into the valley below. As the first of, Turner's Tunnels, 180 meters of tunnel, hand carved out of rock came into view they knew the worst was over. As a child Saoirse had loved this tunnel with its hole in the roof that marked the border between Kerry and Cork. It was a regular feature of their annual summer holiday day trip to West Cork. One of her favourite memories was rolling the car windows down and roaring her head off and then waiting for the echo. It was a different story entering it on a bike though. Knowing that Saoirse always felt a little disorientated with the light change Oisin reminded her "Don't forget to turn on your light Saoirse. Remember it will take a few seconds for your eyes to adjust from light to darkness. Focus on the light from the exit, it will show you where you are aiming for." "The light at the end of the tunnel" she said nervously. He smiled, and blowing her a quick kiss he said, "no matter, what happens in there stay focused on the end of the tunnel, and get out of there in one piece." "Oisin have you lost it or what, what's going to happen?" "I don't know" he replied, "but I have a bad feeling." At that she laughed. "You and your feelings" she said. "I promise to stay focused and not look up to the roof" she joked. "I'm serious Saoirse, but let's go and we can have a good holler and see how good our echo is today."

As they were exiting the tunnel Oisin slowed down. "Phew" Saoirse said "we made it out in one piece. What was all that about back there Oisin." "Never mind, I was wrong about something" he said "I have to swap the water bottles, why don't you ride on and I will catch up?" Saoirse was a little puzzled as to what was going on, he seemed to be acting a bit strange all of a sudden. She rode on anyways because she knew he would catch up as he was much better on the descent than she was. She was a good climber but was overly careful on the descent. She would never make a racer and she knew that. While Oisin had said nothing to Saoirse he had a sense that Donal had been trailing them all day, since Castletownbere. A few times as they were climbing when he looked back, he thought he recognised him a couple of riders back. Based on his power on the bike Oisin had been expecting him to pass them since Castletownbere, and in particular on the climb from Glengarriff. Oisin knew he hadn't passed yet as he had been keeping an eye out for him.

Deep in his gut, Oisin felt there was something off with Donal. He couldn't quite put his finger on it. He knew what it looked like on the surface to Saoirse. She thought Donal was only baiting himself for the rise. But he felt there was something slightly unhinged with Donal. One of the life lessons his mother had instilled in him as a child was trust your gut. Never rationalise it. If it's telling you something is off, then it generally is. She used to call it his safety radar. Up to this point in his life it had generally served him well and he felt now was no different. Every time he met Donal his safety radar was going into overdrive and he couldn't deny that. He didn't know how to put words on it to explain it to Saoirse. He didn't want to scare Saoirse, she would probably think he was over-reacting and say he was just going all alpha male or something like that. Anyways he had said his piece coming out of Castletownbere and she had totally dismissed it. He had half expected Donal to appear in the tunnel, so it did not surprise him when Donal turned up behind him as he was taking off from the Tunnel. Donal greeted him with an overly cheery "How's it going man, have you lost her?" "I have not, she is just there in front of us." "Look Oisin," Donal said, "I know I have been giving you a hard time, but I do wish you both the best together." "Whatever" Oisin said not trusting him in the slightest and pushing on downhill.

From behind Oisin heard "Oh shit" and the screech of breaks before he felt a huge impact take his back wheel out from under him. His own bike began careering towards the side of the road. In that instant he knew he was coming off. With good reaction he unclipped his shoes as he was tossed onto the road, sliding on the tar before landing on the grassy bank with a weight on top of him. He was stunned for a moment, it had happened so fast, he couldn't grasp exactly what happened. He was in agony. His left hip and shoulder felt like they were on fire and there was a weight on top of him. The weigh he realised was another person. "Jesus Christ" he said as he realised it was Donal. At that he found his voice saying "For fuck sake man, this is really taking things too far... are you fucking trying to kill me or what?" With his free hand he took a swipe at Donal who groaned as he tried to move.

Saoirse having heard the noise of the crash stopped. She waited for a minute or two wondering why Oisin had not caught up to her. She decided to go back to where the crash was. Others were starting to gather there so she thought Oisin would probably be there trying to help out. She couldn't believe her eyes when she got closer and realised the two injured people were Oisin and Donal. All she could think of was, who knocked whom. She immediately assumed the worst of the two men.

She could see they were both in agony. Oisin looked liked he had skid across the ground, his shorts and t-shirt were torn, and he was a mess. Donal on the other hand didn't look too good either, he seemed to be contorting with pain. Ignoring everyone standing around she waded in. "God all mighty, ye two amadáns" she yelled at them, "even for ye, this is really taking it too far. What the hell happened?" At this point everyone who had gathered were staring at her speechless. She continued seemingly unaware of her audience. "I can't believe the two of ye. Look at the state of ye. Ye are like two children fighting over a toy. This has gone way too far though." "For fuck sake Saoirse, for once will you shut up, can't you see we are both hurt here," Oisin growled. Simmering down she asked, "what happened to ye?" "He clipped me," Oisin said. "I did not, well I did, but not in the way he means it, I promise Saoirse," Donal groaned. "I didn't do it on purpose. Someone else bumped me." "Where are they so now?" Oisin roared at him. "All I can see is the two of us." Saoirse, recovering from the initial fright and the burst of adrenaline, said, "lads I don't know what happened, but neither of you will be cycling home from here. I had better call the emergency team."

At that point another cyclist stepped forward saying, "I already called them before you got here." "Thank you but did you by any chance see what happened?" she asked. "No" he said. "I just saw them go down and it didn't look good, so I pulled up and called the emergency number." Saoirse looked around, and said, "Does anyone have water and some tissues? Maybe we could help them to get cleaned up a bit while we wait." Seeing that the drama was over, a lot of people moved off to finish their own cycles. Tissues and water were found and jackets were handed to her to keep the lads warm while they waited for the ambulance.

Just then she noticed Donal's knee. It seemed to be twisted and he clearly was in agony. "Donal" she said gently "are you OK?" He gripped her hand saying, "Saoirse I think I am going to pass out or get sick with the pain." Holding his hand, she said "just hang in there until the ambulance comes and we will get you out of here." He weakly smiled his thanks. "Oisin" he said hoarsely though the pain. " I didn't clip you on purpose... believe me, someone else hit me first." "If you say so" Oisin said. Saoirse took Oisin's hand with her other one saying, "where are you hurt?" "My, mmmy ssshoulder and hhhip are on fffire" he said as he began to shake with shock. Turning to the few remaining onlookers, she said with tears in her eyes, "I need help , we need to keep them warm, while they wait." One older lady stepped forward with two foil blankets from her carrier bag. "Here you go love," she said. "I always carry them, I'm a nurse, can I help?" Leaving go of Donal's hand, Saoirse said, "Can you please look after him? I need to look after my fiancée, here." With that she wrapped the blanket around Oisin and held him as best she could without hurting him. "Oisin" she said, "please stay with me." She could feel him shaking, but they had to wait. With the body heat from her his shaking subsided a little but he was only just lucid. She was getting scared. Luckily the two ambulances arrived at roughly the same time from either direction and taking one look at the lads, the paramedics loaded Oisin first and then Donal. Saoirse decided she had enough of the day and would go back with Oisin. Lucky for her she did because after the fright she was in no condition herself to cycle back. She wasn't even sure if she would be able to drive Oisin's car back from Kenmare. She decided she would call her Dad and Sean to see if either of them would come over and help her bring the car and bikes back.

After the first ring her dad answered the phone: "Saoirse what is it?" When she heard his voice, she burst out crying. "Saoirse are you OK pet?" her dad asked again in a worried voice. She eventually got it out: "Dad, I need you to collect me in Kenmare, Oisin came off his bike." "Is he hurt?" her dad asked gently, "are you OK?" Pulling herself together, she said "I'm fine, he is destroyed, the ambulance is taking him to the hospital." "Where are you?" her dad asked. "In the ambulance too, but they will drop me in Kenmare. Can you bring Sean to drive Oisin's car back, I don't think I can at the moment?" "Saoirse pet, hang in there, we will be over straight away."

On the way back in the car with her Dad, Saoirse said, "Dad I have something to tell you." "What is it love?" "Oisin and I have moved in together, we are getting married." "Ah Saoirse, I'm delighted for ye, he is a lovely lad, a bit hot headed, but he is mad about you. He has been for years, you know." "What! He has not, we were just friends.""I know ye were, but he loved you all the same." "Tell me more Dad, how did you know?" "There are many ways of showing someone you love them. You don't have to be hopping in and out of bed with someone to love them you know. He has been in love with you my girl since the day he met you." "He has not" she argued. "He has, I knew it the first time I saw ye together. I said that's the man that will marry my daughter. Mind you it's taken ye longer than I thought to get there, but ye have all the same." That's mad and you never mentioned it." "It wasn't my place. Out of curiosity, what was it that changed things?" "I was seeing someone else for a while" she replied. "Funny that" he said "nothing like a bit of competition to wake a lad up."

"How are we going to break it to Mom?" she asked. "Yerrah don't worry about her, she will come around to the idea." "She isn't mad about him, is she though Dad?" "Ah she just thought he was a bit cocky and when he broke her window that was the final straw." Pulling into her driveway he said, "Leave it to me, and I will have a chat with her and then the two of ye call around when he is OK again. She will be grand." Leaning over she kissed him on the forehead saying, "Thanks Dad, do you want to come in for a cup of tea?" "No love, my supper will be on the table when I get home … If you need me for anything else give me a shout." "Thanks again Dad" she said, getting out of the car. He winked at her; "Don't mention it, and don't worry about your mom, she will come round to the idea in her own time, but make sure and don't leave it too long to call over."

CHAPTER 18

Life is too short, we can't live ours to fulfil someone else's dream

After a shower and some food Saoirse decided to check on the lads and see how they were doing. Oisin answered the phone on the first ring. "Hi Ois" Saoirse said. "How are you doing? Will they keep you in?" "No" he said, "I will be left home tonight, Padraig is picking me up. I only have surface wounds, it looked and felt worse than it was." "Thank God, for that", she replied "and here was I thinking I might be getting a cripple for a husband" she joked. "No" he replied "you are safe enough, they just cleaned and dressed the grazing and gave me a fine dose of painkillers, so I will be back in action again soon. I am just waiting for the doctor to call round to let me go home." "Do you know what happened to Donal?" he asked. "I don't, I was going to text him next," she replied. She hung up from Oisin and texted Donal. "*Hey how u doing*?" He immediately replied: "*Just been for scan, cruciate ligament ruptured, will need reconstruction surgery*." Her phone pinged again immediately after: "*Did not crash into Oisin on purpose, was clipped 1st.*" She replied, "*Sorry to hear, hope all goes well, anything I can do 2 help?*" "*Nothing, just believe me.*"

As the evening wore on Saoirse was in a state of shock herself and also disappointment. They had planned to stay in Kenmare and enjoy the after race festivities. It usually was great fun, with everyone on a high after finishing. This all seemed surreal though. She couldn't believe that potentially the two lads were hurt because of her. She really didn't think that she was such a bad judge of character. But if Donal actually had clipped Oisin on purpose then she was a very bad judge of character, and he was potentially dangerous. Maybe Oisin was right... maybe he had a screw loose somewhere. She kept asking herself though, if he had meant to hurt Oisin how had he come off so badly from the accident himself? In her gut, she felt she should believe him. From what she knew of him other than winding Oisin up he had seemed to be genuine enough. In her heart she felt he was not the dangerous type.

Later that night, Oisin came home exhausted and sore despite the painkillers. As he came in, she reached out to hold him, but he caught her hands fearing she would hurt him. She reached up on tip toe and kissed him on the lips, saying "you look sore." He simply whispered, "I am, I really need to go to bed and lie down." She came in and sat on the bed beside him and just held his good hand.

"Oisin, what do you actually think happened?" "You know Saoirse, I have been thinking of nothing else all evening, but I think he might be telling the truth. Before he hit me, I heard a bike slide and I think I heard him shout something." Thank God she said to herself not wanting to think the worst of Donal, after all she had slept with him. She didn't want to think she had been in bed with a mad man. "Oisin I can see you are worn out, I will leave you for a rest, if you need anything just give me a shout," she said. She leaned over and gently kissed him before leaving the room.

Back in the kitchen she texted Donal *"U r forgiven, Oisin believes u." "But do u?"* he replied. She pondered on that for a moment, what did she actually believe? Then she replied, *"if he does, I do." "Thanks, it's ur opinion that counts 2 me."* That's strange she thought, she might as well spell it out for him for once and for all. *"U know, this is it, we r finished, I'm getting married 2 Oisin."* He replied, " *good luck, c u around.*" She hoped not for a while, but she knew it was a definite possibility as Killarney is a small town. She knew that if Oisin had not declared his love, she would probably still be with Donal. In her heart she felt he was a good guy. She knew he was the type her mother had hoped she would meet, wealthy, with property and that she could be a kept wife. The irony of the situation was not lost on her. Oisin right now had neither wealth nor property and she would probably be working to keep the two of them in her home for the first few years of their marriage. She knew however Oisin was the right choice for her, he was her soul mate. She knew the time had come, they would have to face her mother tomorrow if Oisin was able, even if he wasn't, she would go herself. She texted her *"Mom, if it's okay, I would like to bring someone to dinner tomorrow."* Her mother replied *"of course your friends are always welcome."* There was no backing out now.

A sore, subdued Oisin sat to the Sunday dinner table in Saoirse's house. Saoirse held his hand under the table in silent moral support. Her father said, "sit down Joan, these two have something to tell you." "I will not," Saoirse's mother replied "until I have the dinner out, then they can tell me what they like." Oh no thought Saoirse this is not going to go well. Her dad said "Oisin lad, how are you feeling after yesterday, you look a bit stiff?" "To tell the truth Dan it's not too bad, it actually looks worse than it is, I got off reasonably lightly." "I just can't understand why anyone would want to go out of their way to cycle them distances. It's crazy." Saoirse's mother said, butting in. "I have told Saoirse here," she continued, "that she would be better off out looking for a good husband, than wandering around the road on that blooming bike, killing herself." "Ah Mom" Saoirse said, "will you leave it off." "I will not" Joan replied, "look at the state he is in, he could have been killed, and then where would ye be?" As she sat down, she said, "Now, what is it, that has brought the two of you over here today? I assume it was not to show off your injuries, so what was it?"

"Mom, Oisin and I are getting married" Saoirse simply stated. "What?" her mother replied. "I thought you two were 'just friends', when did that change?" "Only recently," Saoirse replied truthfully. Oisin squeezed her hand under the table. Her mother blew out a breath, shaking her head, she said "It took ye long enough to figure it out, didn't it? To tell ye the truth, I had my suspicions all along, but I went along with the 'friends' bit. Well congratulations" she said. "Let me get out the bubbly, and toast, to you and Oisin." This took Saoirse by surprise, she had expected more resistance from her mother. It was going a lot better than she had hoped. "When is the big day going to be?" her mother asked. "We are planning to get married in September." "That's a lovely time of year," her mother replied, "the weather is usually nice. Where will ye have it?" Saoirse felt Oisin squeezing her hand as she replied, "in Oisin's garden, we are going to put up a marquee for the ceremony and renovate the barn there for the reception."

At that her mother jumped up from the chair. "No daughter of mine is getting married in a tent and a shed" she said. "What will the neighbours think Dan?" she cried. "That we couldn't afford to give her a proper wedding ... you are not getting married in a shed and that's that." "Ah Joan give them a chance" her father said, "it's their day, things have changed, people are getting married all over the place nowadays, hear them out." Turing to face him she said, "my only daughter is not getting married in a shed and that is that." At this point Saoirse said, "Mom, we don't want to upset you, but we are getting married in Oisin's garden this September and that's it." "This September! How in the name of God will you be ready by then, that's only 4 months away? I thought you meant next year … What's the hurry anyway? Are you pregnant or what?" she asked. "I am not" Saoirse replied, "and there is plenty of time to organise a simple wedding for September." "Simple" her mother spat out, "is this what he has reduced you to? A cheep little shotgun wedding, I had expected more for my daughter." "That's enough" Saoirse said as she stood pulling Oisin up with her. "I don't know why I thought you might be happy for me this time. We will be getting married in September with or without you and that's final." With that, Saoirse and Oisin walked out of the house.

As they walked down the driveway towards the car, Saoirse looked back and saw her Dad at the door. His head was bowed as he waved to her. Saoirse said "poor Dad" and ran back to give him a hug. "I'm sorry Dad," she said, "I don't know how you put up with her." He hugged her to him, and laughed, saying, "she will come round Saoirse, you know her, she always does." Saoirse hugged him back saying, "I know, but why does she have to ruin everything first? What is wrong with her, why for once can't she be happy for me? Why is she always trying to control everything? " "Oh, Saoirse, I don't know," he sighed, "I hate to see ye fighting like this though." "You know Dad, she never once came to any of my football games or never once cheered for me at the finish line of any of my cycles, it's like she can't accept who I am." "Oh Saoirse love, she loves you, but she just doesn't get that you have your life and she can't accept that she can't live hers through yours. She had a difficult childhood and when you arrived, she placed all her hopes and dreams on your little shoulders." "It hurts Dad that I am such a disappointment... I'm not the daughter she wanted." "Oh, Saoirse love, no one would be able to fulfil her ideals, you are you and she is herself … I am very proud of you and I will be happy to walk you down any aisle. Oisin is a good man and he loves you." "Thanks Dad, I love you." "Run on love," he said, "Oisin is waiting for you... and don't worry about Mom. Give her some time to come around. She will you know."

CHAPTER 19

The seed of our future is often planted when we are young

Oisin's mom was in great form, it was the evening of her garden party. Everything was ready and she was really looking forward to celebrating Oisin and Saoirse's engagement. She still couldn't understand how they had wasted so many years, but she accepted that this was just the way of the youth of today. She was looking forward to meeting Saoirse's parents as well. Over the years she had gotten the sense from Oisin that Saoirse's mom was a bit of a battle axe, but she would reserve that judgement until she met the woman in person. She knew that if Saoirse was anything to go by, they had reared her well at least.

She acknowledged to herself that she was absolutely thrilled that Oisin was going to take over the running of the farm and the garden. It was about time that Tom and herself had a bit of a break after rearing the lot of them. She knew that Saoirse would be a great support for Oisin. The wedding at home would be the icing on the cake. It would be her ultimate garden party. She knew that Oisin was a bit worried about the finances, between the wedding and expanding the business. Tom and herself would help them out with that. In her opinion the farm shop was genius. Secretly she was delighted that it was the garden aspect of the business that he really wanted to develop. Oisin had always loved the garden as a child and she had always fostered his interest in it. The rest of the lads had preferred to be out on the farm with the tractors and animals but not Oisin, he had always loved planting and growing. She knew mothers should not have favourites, but Oisin really had a special place in her heart, both as her baby and as the child who had the same interests she had. She decided that she would give him the money to put in one of them big industrial tunnels. If he was going to do this, he may as well do it right and that would be her wedding present to him.

She chuckled as she remembered the evening he had told her about the barn and the country and western-themed wedding. She had loved it immediately; he had always been her little free spirit and liked to do things a little differently. That wedding would certainly be different. He had thought of it all. The bar counter for the wedding could be the shop counter later in the farm shop and they would be able to hang things like onions and garlic from the overhead beams. The building itself would be absolutely fabulous. She could see it all as he had described it, white washed walls, the big sliding red door, the two cart wheel windows. It would be fabulous. She had every faith in Padraig and his team pulling it off in time for the wedding.

She had been so excited about Oisin finally getting engaged that she had invited all the cousins and friends to the party. She admitted tonight would be more like a wedding party than an engagement party but in her excitement, she had invited everyone. She felt it would be a great night and the beginnings of her own next phase in life. She had relented on the alcoholic drink, for one night, but she hoped that it wouldn't get too rowdy. It would be a right session tonight, though. She told all the cousins to bring their instruments and Tom had put a floor down outside in the yard so they could dance a set or two. She hoped that Saoirse's parents wouldn't be too intimidated by the madness, but she loved a good party... It would start at six pm in order to get the food out of the way and then they could get on with the music and dancing.

With everything ready and the first of the guests already here she was keeping an eye out for Oisin and Saoirse. When she saw them come up the driveway, she called for a bit of hush. As they stepped out of the car, she said, "let's toast the newly engaged couple." "To Oisin and Saoirse. I am delighted to finally be welcoming you Saoirse officially into the family. You already have been a part of our lives for the past few years but it's official now." Saoirse a little embarrassed by all the attention said,

"Thank you, Geraldine, it's been my pleasure, it looks like you have truly outdone yourself tonight." "Ah now my Oisin," his mother continued, "I am delighted you finally opened your eyes to this fine woman and decided to make her your wife." To everyone else present, she said "enjoy the night, the food is waiting for ye and let's make this a night to remember."

As Oisin's mom was making her speech, Saoirse's parents arrived. Saoirse's mom, not still having fully come to terms with the whole idea, was there because it was important to be seen. As she entered, she said to her husband, "They are a common lot Dan, could she not have done better for herself? Imagine an engagement party outside in the yard, like this. Look over there, that must be the shed that they are going to have the wedding in. What is the world coming to? … my daughter getting married in a shed," she muttered. "No Joan, they are good country folk" Dan said, "and Saoirse and Oisin are very happy together. He is a good man and whether they get married in a church or the field over there we will be at it." "Well, I think it's all very common, and I'm entitled to my opinion" she huffed. Saoirse's father sighed; "Well Joan, I don't want to be arguing with you, but as you said she is your only daughter, and she is my only one too. Let's put a smile on our faces and enjoy the night, for what it is …. our daughter's engagement party. Once Saoirse and Oisin are happy together surley that's all that counts?"

Out of the corner of her eye Saoirse spotted her mother and her heart leaped. So, she has come, she thought to herself. In that instant Saoirse decided she would let her mother apologise to her first. This once, she would not do the running. This was her night, and she was not going to be running around worrying about what her mother was thinking or who she might upset. She loved Oisin, and Geraldine and Tom along with the rest of Oisin's siblings had always made her welcome. She had often wished that her family were a little bit more like Oisin's. She knew it was most likely that her dad had convinced her mom to come. It could also be the fact she was worried about what the neighbours would say. In particular if they heard she hadn't attended her own daughter's engagement party that convinced her to come in the end. She knew her mother would be judging everyone here tonight and would have an opinion on them all tomorrow. Thinking about it now Saoirse just felt sorry for her.

Oisin sensed the change in Saoirse and following her gaze he said, "I see they've come." She shrugged her shoulders saying, "yes they are here." He lent over and whispered "Saoirse, this is our party, let's enjoy it, you have nothing to prove to her." He then kissed her gently on the lips and said, "I love you as you are, remember that." She smiled her thanks, up at him, but he could see the hurt still lingered in her eyes. Taking her hand, he said "Come on let's meet our guests, this is our party, don't let her ruin it."

"By the way, I never told you how beautiful you look tonight," he whispered for distraction. "I think you showed me... but do tell me again" she sighed. "That dress is absolutely stunning on you. You look good enough to eat he murmured" as he nuzzled her neck. "Stop that," she muttered "they are all watching us." " I am just letting them all know," he said smiling at her, "that I am the lucky man here with you tonight." It was a fragile solid gold chain with a gold drop bar that dripped into her cleavage. "By the way this necklace is some piece where did you get it? Is it real?" "Thank you Oisin, it's fabulous, I never got to thank you earlier for it. I think it's amazing with this dress." he looked at her puzzled. "What are you talking about Saoirse? I didn't buy it." In response to his statement, she felt a shiver creep up her spine. "Oisin this is not a joke. I thought you left it for me as an engagement present." "What do you mean?" he paused and took a step back? "Saoirse I love you but we are planning for a wedding and trying to set up a business, that thing cost an arm and a leg. I assure you I didn't buy it." "How did it get there so?" Get where? Where did you find it?" At that he took both her hands and turned her to him. "Oisin I found it on the hall table inside the front door. It was wrapped up in a beautiful gift box and I assumed you had left it for me." "Saoirse even if I had why would I leave it on the hall table? I can assure you, if I had bought you that, I would have given it to you in person and probably while you had nothing on." She could see he was irate now and also concerned. "Was there anything with it," he asked, cautiously. "A note that said 'our moments forever cherished,'" she said shakily. "I did think that didn't sound like you, but I was blown away by the piece." "God all mighty Saoirse, I give you one guess where that came from," he said angrily. "He is escalating. Do you think he knew tonight was the engagement party?" "I don't" Saoirse said honestly "but it wouldn't have been hard to find out on Facebook." "He never would, have come into the house Oisin, though would he?" she asked shakily. "Well someone did, I told you he was mad, and we also know he is dangerous. I think we are going to have to go to the guards tomorrow and report this." "What will I do with the necklace?" she asked ripping it from her neck. "Oisin, I feel dirty, it's like his finger has been between my breasts all night." "My god" she shivered, "we won't even be able to look at our engagement photos, that necklace is like having him in them too" she cried. She shivered again, "Oisin it's like I can't get away from him. He keeps finding a way to hang on to me. God I was such a bad judge of character", she said with tears in her eyes. "Saoirse it's ok, we will sort it out, together" Oisin assured her.

"Oisin I'm afraid now, who was in my house today, it couldn't have been him, he must be on crutches. Who did he get to drop it off? What if after all he is into some sort of dealing and that IT nonsense was just that. Maybe you were right, he could be dangerous. It makes me wonder now all them stories he told me about Martha his ex. How much of that was true?" "I don't know about her, but we need to make sure we get him out of our lives, and it might not be easy with the money he has." "How are we going to do that?" "We start with a statement to the guards tomorrow," he stated decisively. "I don't know Oisin, it all sounds a bit nuts, what will we tell them? I slept with some fella and now he is stalking me." "Yes, that was the start of it." he replied. "But Oisin when they ask for proof what have we got?" "He sent flowers, turned up at my door, was in a crash with you and sent me a present on the day of my engagement party. I don't know Oisin that, that would stand up anywhere. You also did all them things apart from not give me a present on our engagement day and I'm not accusing you of stalking me" "Well the present was breaking and entering", he said. "Not if the door had been left slightly open, I had only gone around the back to water the flowers, so I had left it open." "I don't know Oisin, if we have a case here." "Saoirse I'm telling you he is not right in the head, but I can't make you do anything about it, if you chose not to."

"Saoirse I actually think it's me he has it in for. I think in his warped way, he might love you, and I just got in his way. But you never know." At that she felt herself shivering again. "Oisin, I read somewhere" she said nervously "that most women murder victims are murdered by their partners or ex-partners." Pulling her into his arms he said, "Let's not go that far. We will start by talking to the guards tomorrow and see what they have to say. Who knows he may even have a previous history? That story you told me about his ex seemed a little far fetched. There might even be something on record there. Tonight, is our night, let's park it if we can and try and enjoy our party." He smiled and said, "and here was me thinking that your mother was our biggest problem." "We haven't crossed that bridge either yet," she said in reply, smiling up at him and taking his hand said, "let's get some food before it gets cold."

As they were queuing at the table for food, her dad joined them saying, "Saoirse love, you look fabulous tonight." Thanks Dad," "I hope you enjoy your night. Your mom also came." "I know" Saoirse replied, "I saw ye coming in." "Will you not come over and say hello" he asked. "I will later, Dad." "Saoirse, she is sorry for the last day and it cost her a lot to come tonight, will you meet her halfway?" "For you Dad, I will. You know Dad I don't hold a grudge, I just want her to be happy for me this once." "Saoirse she is delighted you are getting married. She was telling all her friends during the week that you had met someone." Oisin's mom from her vantage point could see something was upsetting Saoirse and decided to interject, "Hi I'm Oisin's mom, you must be Saoirse's Dad. It's lovely to meet you finally, I have heard a lot about you over the years." "And I you," Saoirse's Dad said in reply. Saoirse left them too it and wandered off to chat with some of Oisin's sisters and sister in laws. She felt really at home with his family.

Once the food was cleared up, his mother instructed the musicians to get going.

Saoirse and Oisin loved to dance and they only left the floor to get a drink or have a breather. During one of her breathers her mom approached her. "Saoirse, I can see you are enjoying yourself. That's good. It's a great night." Saoirse was dumbstruck. Her mother continued "I was talking to Oisin's Dad earlier and he was singing your praises. He's a lovely man" she said. Saoirse looked at her wondering how much drink she had. "I know it's only outside in the yard, but Geraldine is a great hostess she has kept me topped up all night. They do know how to let their hair down don't they? I hadn't expected it to be much fun, especially a party out in a yard … Saoirse maybe you are right, the wedding in the shed might be alright." Saoirse was completely taken aback. Was her mother actually giving her, her blessing for once, she wondered. "They are a bit rough and wild, but I think they are good people," her mother continued. Jesus Saoirse thought to herself, that's high praise, she must really have hit the bottle. "Thanks," Saoirse said, "I'm glad you are enjoying the night." "Before you go" her mother said, "can I ask you two things?" "Sure, ask away." "Are you pregnant?" "No Mom" Saoirse said resignedly. "Why are you asking me that Mom?" "Well it all still seems to be a bit hurried. Do you love him?" "I do" Saoirse said smiling. "I think I always have." "That's good, at least it's not a shotgun wedding and you are not just settling for him …" Joan paused and hesitated for a second before saying, "There is still time to change your mind, you know, if you wanted to, I thought you would do a bit better than him..." "Ah Mom, I just told you I love him and I am going to marry him, I would do it tonight if I could." "Right so" her mother said, "all I'm saying is there is no need to be so hasty, don't you know what they say?" "Yeah I know, 'marry in haste, repent at leisure', but it hardly applies to us after all this time?" "Saoirse it's your life, I have said my piece, now I must find your Dad."

Saoirse just stood there gobsmacked. She knew her mother had raised her, but she seemed to be the most emotionally unavailable person she knew. She couldn't believe she had asked her them questions tonight. Imagine telling her there was time to leave him at her engagement party. She knew she would never understand her mother and that was mutual. Just then Margaret sidled up beside her and wrapped her arms around her saying "I have to hand it to Oisin's mom she does throw a cracking party." She does Saoirse replied. "Everything OK? You seem a bit subdued." Margaret asked. "Ah Margaret it's all mental," Saoirse blurted out. "Oisin thinks Donal is a fruit cake, who is stalking me. My mom was trying to get me to reconsider my engagement, she was even giving me her own version of relationship advice." Hang on there Saoirse, rewind a little to the stalking bit. That's serious. You said Oisin thinks, but what do you think?" "To be honest I don't know, what I think at the moment, but I really don't like the fact that someone was in my house today without permission. Then I think maybe it was innocent enough the door was open and whom ever it was just dropped it on the hall table." "What make's you think it was from him?" "The note and the fact that it was really expensive, no one I know would have bought it. I think. I originally thought it was a romantic gesture from Oisin..." Saoirse trailed off. "Saoirse for what it's worth, you have told me a few times yourself that there was some inconsistencies with him, 'socially challenged' was how I think you put it." "I know, but I still can't quite believe that there would be badness in him." "I think on this one, I would go with Oisin and make that statement," Margaret advised. "Do you really think so Margaret? I just feel like a total fool." "Look Saoirse, bad things happen to women all the time, many of them cannot quite pin down their starting point. You're lucky this has not gotten out of hand yet... at least if you call the station, they will have your story on record, if something happens. I'm not saying that anything will, but if something did, they would probably react quicker. Whatever has happened you have to stop second guessing yourself, it is not your fault" "You know, Margaret, I might just make that report. I suppose it's just hurt pride really" Margaret gave her a friendly squeeze and added, "Remember it's not your fault, you did nothing wrong, you took him at face value, now put a smile on your face and enjoy what little is left of you're night. We will be off now ourselves, as we will have an early start with the kids tomorrow." "Thanks Margaret," Saoirse said, "thanks for everything."

As the party drew to a close Oisin and Saoirse left by taxi. "Saoirse it was a cracking party wasn't it? … Mom really does know how to throw a good party." He squeezed her hand, continuing "We will sort out this Donal thing, you know. I was talking to one of the lads tonight. He is a guard. He said, make a statement and at least there will be something on record." I suppose so she replied, I also talked to Margaret and she said the same thing, it just all still seems a bit weak to me." I know Saoirse but it's better to be safe than sorry. I'm glad your parents came tonight. Your Dad is sound, and your mother does love you too in her own strange way." "I'm not so sure" Saoirse replied. "Ah I think she does. Do you know what she said to me? Look after my daughter the way her father looked after me and you won't go too far wrong." With that Saoirse had tears in her eyes. "It's true," Oisin went on, "she said he has always looked after her like she was the queen. Saoirse I love you, for you, I know who you are. I'm sorry your mother upsets you but you are an amazing woman. Despite all her carry on, you have never let her hold you back, don't let her ruin our wedding for you." "Ah Oisin I know, it usually doesn't get to me. It's just this once I wanted to have a mom who would go wedding dress shopping, help plan menus and just share this journey with me, without criticising everything." "I know Si, I am sorry," he said comforting her. "Oisin, I know it's mad, I will have to accept it because she won't change now, it just hurts that's all." "It's true what she said about your Dad though," Oisin replied, "If I can be half as good a husband as him, I wouldn't be doing too bad." "To tell you the truth Oisin, he is great, but I would prefer our relationship to be based on equality. We have never tip toed around each other and let's not start now. It just wouldn't work." He smiled at her. "That's my Saoirse, cut through the crap and say it like it is." "Oisin I think we will have our ups and downs but we will get there. We love each other and that's all that matters, we can work out the rest. She leaned forward and said "Can I have a kiss from my Fiancée? After tonight it's real." He leaned over and kissed her deeply. She sighed and leaned back into him saying, "I can't wait to get you home for tonight." He laughed. "Now you're talking." She smiled and taking his hand in hers said, "To me and you and whatever the future holds …"

About the Author

Hello my name is Máire O' Leary. I grew up loving books in a house with no television. As a child I visited the library fortnightly and always dreamed of having my name on a book cover. 'Freewheeling to Love' has fulfilled that dream for me.

I am at my happiest in the great outdoor's and living in Killarney, Co. Kerry I am blessed with easy access to wonderful lakes, mountains, rivers and the beach. A good day out for me is a day spent with my husband and two boys in nature.

In my day job I am a Health Promotion Officer with Cork Kerry Community Healthcare. For the past 16 years I have predominantly worked in the field of Sexual Health Promotion.

'Freewheeling to Love' started out as something to entertain myself during my first maternity leave 7 years ago. Covid lockdown inspired me to finish it. It has been a labour of love for me. I sincerely hope you enjoy reading it as much as I did writing it.

Please Review

Dear Reader,

If you enjoyed this book, would you kindly post a short review on Goodreads? Your feedback will make all the difference to getting the word out about this book.

Thank you in advance.